For Shannon and Chip
and Brandon Cole (May 17, 1998-   )

About Rick Carroll

Author and travel writer Rick Carroll is a former daily journalist for the *San Francisco Chronicle*. He later covered Hawai'i and the Pacific for United Press International with a Nikon and a notebook.

His self-illustrated articles on Rapa Nui (Easter Island) and Huahine (Society Islands), have won the Lowell Thomas Award of the Society of American Travel Writers and the Gold Award of the Pacific Asia Travel Association. His reports from Manila and the Southern Philippines during the Marcos era won a national Headliner's Award.

Hawai'i's Best Spooky Tales 2 is Carroll's third collection of true accounts of inexplicable encounters in the Islands. He has shared these stories with audiences throughout the islands through personal appearances at schools, libraries, bookstores, and conferences. He was a 1997 Visiting Artist on Lāna'i and performed at the Bankoh Talk Story Festival on O'ahu.

He is also the author of six guidebooks, including *Great Outdoor Adventures of Hawaii*. His next book, *Travelers' Tales Hawaii*, an anthology of personal discoveries in the Hawaiian Islands, is due in 1999.

Carroll lives in Lanikai, on O'ahu's windward side, and spends his summers in Friday Harbor, Washington.

HAWAI'I'S BEST SPOOKY TALES 2

MORE TRUE LOCAL SPINE-TINGLERS

COLLECTED BY
RICK CARROLL

THE
BESS
PRESS

3565 Harding Ave, Honolulu, Hawai'i 96816
(808) 734-7159 fax (808) 732-3627 www.besspress.com

Design: Carol Colbath
Moon logo from a design by Kevin Hand
Cover photo: Courtesy Hawaiʻi State Archives

Library of Congress Cataloging-in-Publication Data

Carroll, Rick
    Hawaii's best spooky tales 2 : more true local
spine-tinglers / collected by Rick Carroll.
        p.   cm.
    Includes illustrations.
    ISBN 1-57306-040-2
    1. Ghost stories, American – Hawaii.
2. Tales – Hawaii. 3. Legends – Hawaii.
I. Title.
GR580.H3.C371 1998   398.25-dc20

Printed in the United States of America

ISBN 1-57306-040-2

Acknowledgments

Some years ago, when the first volume of this trilogy was published, a Honolulu bookstore owner innocently asked, "Are the authors local? The answer, as you know, is definitely yes!

This book, like its two predecessors, is a collection of first-person stories by predominantly local authors, most of them never before published, all of them accomplished storytellers in Hawai'i's chicken-skin genre.

Their personal accounts give the books an authentic soul and create a body of evidence that leads you to believe something is going on out there that nobody can explain. I thank each and every contributing author for sharing stories that might otherwise never have seen print.

No book, especially an anthology, is a solitary effort, and for this latest volume, *Hawai'i's Best Spooky Tales 2*, I gratefully acknowledge and thank Benjamin Bess for his fostering of local publishing in Hawai'i and the Pacific; my painstaking editor, Revé Shapard; and designer Carol Colbath for capturing night marchers on the cover.

I thank my wife, Marcie, for enduring my late-night distractions, and finally, I thank you, the ardent reader, for making the books local best-sellers.

Mahalo nui loa,

Rick Carroll

Table of Contents

Introduction

" . . . *the marchers carried candlenut torches which burned brightly even on a rainy night. They might be seen even in broad daylight and were followed by whirlwinds . . . a heavy downpour of rain, with mist, thunder and lightning, or heavy seas . . .* "

—Mary Kawena Pukui,
"The Marchers of the Night"

Beware, but do not be afraid of the spirits of the *ali'i*. Our *huaka'i o ka pō*, or night marchers, are meant not to frighten, only remind you that at any time, anywhere in Hawai'i, you should expect the unexpected.

We who live here are surrounded day and night by the supernatural. It's in the air everywhere. While most local folks are *akamai* and know their way around a *heiau*, most visitors have no idea what can happen if they don't watch their step. *Kapu* means more than "no trespassing" in Hawai'i.

For the unwary, Hawai'i can be filled with peril; it's no paradise, pal.

If you doubt me, I now offer in evidence this fine collection of true accounts by residents and travelers alike, who experienced and survived extraordinary encounters in the Islands. Things they can't explain. Unreal episodes. Odd events. The inexplicable, mysterious stuff of real and surreal Hawai'i.

A Preview

Hawai'i's Best Spooky Tales 2 features new stories by twenty-seven authors of varied ages, occupations, and ethnic origins, from all islands. Their stories are guaranteed to shiver your bones. I'll give you a brief preview:

- Stephanie Kaluahine Reid thinks the missionary family she sees by the side of the road in "The Lost Family of Honoka'a" is a mirage. It's not.
- Ruben (Lopina) Makua, a former security guard at 'Iolani Palace, sees a royal figure roaming the grounds one night and realizes that it's "Queen Lili'uokalani at the Palace."
- Madelyn Horner Fern receives directions from an unreal fellow traveler on "A Moonless Night in Kona" and describes the haunting of a child in Waimānalo in "Lilia."
- Thomas N. Colbath makes a Pearl Harbor pilgrimage and overhears conversations of long-lost sailors in "*Arizona* Ghosts."
- Doug Self tries to explain what led him to live on a sea cliff in "Mystery on Maui."

These are just a few of the best spooky tales in the Hawaiian Islands I have gathered for your late-night reading pleasure. This sequel, I promise, is as full of chills as its predecessors.

Some stories are so scary you probably shouldn't read them alone, at home, after dark. I am thinking of "The Spirit of Honokāne," by Carolyn Sugiyama Classen; "A Moloka'i Mū Sighting," by Joyce Garnes; "Hale o Olomana," by Jerry and Debby Kermode; and "Oloku'i," by Pam Soderberg.

At least three stories illustrate that few are safe, even at home or at work:

- "The Halloween Cat of Kaimukī," by Alex Cheong Linder, is a strange story about an irrepressible cat at the local library.
- "The *Holoholo* Man," by Richard S. Fukushima, will make you wary of strangers seeking handouts.
- "The Stinky Ghost," by Andrea Hunt Bills, reveals that some old souls make a lingering impression.

Three of Hawai'i's best-known storytellers contributed original stories to this book. Helen Fujie, the legendary story-teller of Lāna'i, now in her 80s, recalls the ominous events that occur when "The Spirits Return to Lāna'i." Nyla Fujii-Babb receives an unsettling reminder of Madame Pele's power in "At the Volcano's Edge." And master storyteller Jeff Gere explains in pidgin what happens "When Kona Winds Blow." His lively stories are available on audiocassettes, O'ahu Spookies #1 and #2. Write, call, or fax 'um at P. O. Box 37495, Honolulu, HI 96837; ph (808) 592-7029; fax (808) 596-7046.

Several stories came from professional writers. Berkeley-based novelist and travel writer Shirley Streshinsky, who frequently visits Hawai'i, tells of her strange aural encounter in "A Kohala Kyrie." Hawai'i-based travel writer Camie Foster takes us on an eerie exploration inside a Hawaiian burial cave on the Big Island of Hawai'i in "A Moment in Time." San Francisco-based author Babs Harrison reveals the truth about a stranger in her bed in "The Spirit of the Lodge." George Fuller's "Is the End Near?," an apocalyptic vision in the velvet embrace of Mauna Kea Resort, is a true spine-tingler, as is Pat Leilani Young's "Connections."

Five of the stories are from Hawai'i public school students: Kaua'i students Amanda Fahselt, Chandelle Rego-Koerte, and Aaron Teves, O'ahu student Crystal Tamayose, and Maui student Ben Lowenthal—a collector of spooky stories himself.

And finally, I invite you to join me "In Kahakuloa," an ancestral valley on Maui's primitive north shore where I learned the hard way a fundamental truth about Polynesia.

A "Thrillogy"

If you like these stories, may I remind you there are others. This is, after all, the third volume of true spooky tales—a "thrillogy" if you will—that began in 1996 with the publication of *Chicken*

Skin: True Spooky Stories of Hawai'i. The total collection now comprises nearly one hundred stories—ample proof that something out of the ordinary is still going on out there.

Spooky stories are as much a part of Hawai'i as the sun and surf. Until now they were whispered on the wind, here and gone like pale shadow tourists. That's why a few years ago, I began collecting stories for others to enjoy. What I never could have guessed then is how well received the stories would be, and not only in Hawai'i.

Acclaim for *Hawai'i's Best Spooky Tales* and its predecessor has come from the most unusual places and in peculiar ways.

Jon (no relation) Carroll, the *San Francisco Chronicle's* favorite daily columnist, wrote of the first volume: "It doesn't matter whether you believe in ghosts and spirits—it's all culture and it's all new."

In 1998, the first two volumes in the series were at or near the top of the *Honolulu Star-Bulletin's* best-seller list. In addition, the books were cited by Hawai'i public librarians as among those most requested by readers of all ages.

Everyone, it seems, has a favorite story. A Maui boy told me he liked "When *Pueo* Gather on Moloka'i" best, then repeated the story almost verbatim.

Others write and tell me they like "Old Pictures," by Ed Chang, or "Night Games," by Tania Leslie and Rich Asprec. Two of my personal favorites are Akoni Akana's "Ghosts of Hula Past" and Lei-Ann Stender Durant's "Three Storms of Hina."

The books inspired a Spooky Tales Talk Story program at O'ahu's Windward Community College, now an annual event. They are kept under lock and key at the Kalihi-Palama Library because many were stolen from shelves by eager young readers. And they have attracted critical praise in Hawai'i and on the mainland. Here's a sample:

"These stories will give you chicken skin. Especially if you read 'em aloud. At night."—Honolulu Advertiser

"Makes you wonder if anyone can avoid encountering the supernatural in Hawai'i."—Native Books and Beautiful Things

" . . . great storytelling . . . part oral history, part memoir, [part] supernatural tales and encounters."
—San Francisco Chronicle

"Engaging anthology . . . a wealth of otherworldly encounters."—Islands Magazine

Both books inspired youthful interest in writing, reading, and storytelling in Hawai'i schools. Teachers like Margaret Grady, of Lahaina, Maui, and Divina Delos Santos, of Lihue, Kaua'i, have used the books to encourage reading and writing in their English classes. What is most heartening, however, is that people of Hawai'i, young and old, are now writing true, first-person spooky stories, and many of you, obviously, are reading them.

The Guide to Spooky Places 2

As a bonus I have added a new, expanded Guide to Spooky Places, with twenty-one more of my favorite historical, cultural, and supernatural sites. You can vicariously enjoy the spooky adventures of others and then go out and experience firsthand that delicious shiver local folks call chicken skin.

Incidentally, should you wonder where our night marchers (on the cover) are going, I suspect they are heading, like our contributing authors, for their nearest bookstore to see how they look in print. So they're probably in a jolly mood. Just the same, be careful out there.

Rick Carroll
Honolulu, Hawai'i

The Island of O'ahu

After dark, 'Iolani Palace seems quiet and peaceful, but night watchmen tell me other-wise. They hear strange noises, but when they search the palace they find nothing awry. But one cool summer night a Hawaiian security guard encounters . . .

Queen Lili'uokalani at the Palace

Sometimes I see dark shadows pass over the palace. Sometimes there are strange noises—footsteps on the stairs, loud sneezes in the basement. Nobody is ever there. Another mystery: the King Street gate is always open. I shut it, it's open. Every time I walk around, the gate is always open. I don't know the reason why. Nobody around. Only me.

I worked as night security guard at the palace twelve years, always the same shift, four to midnight. I no believe in ghosts before until this appeared on me. I not forget the night.

The year was 1986, summertime, about 10:30. I was making my rounds, sometimes going clockwise, sometimes going opposite-wise. You know, change the way, I gotta throw the people off. Sometimes they check me how many times I go around and which way. A lot of homeless people sleep there, I find them sometimes under the trees. Just chase 'em out.

I made my rounds about three times that night, walking around the palace, with flashlight and radio, and I got the feelings. Kept getting a feeling real cold, and I could feel something leaning on me—not heavy, light—something cold right on me, right here on my chest. It was summertime, and I said, "Gee, kinda cool, wonder why?"

When I came to my fourth time around the palace, I

saw her. Straight ahead about twenty feet away. She was looking at me. I was looking at her. I saw her right between the new archive building and the old archive, right in the center, right in the middle. She was facing me. She didn't say anything. When I started moving, she started moving, walking away.

She was dressed all in black, with a black veil over her face. No can see her face, but I knew it was her. Same size as Lili'uokalani. She had that kind bonnet on the back of her head, like on the statue at the state capitol.

She didn't say anything. She was moving. She was not walking. Her gown was not touching the ground. I don't know how to describe it. I did not see her feet, she got to be floating.

I had flashlight and radio. I supposed to call in anything that happens, but to my mind, if I call in, the sergeant figure, you know, this guy's kind of nuts, something li' dat, so I keep it to myself. Guys later told me how come you no shine the flashlight? I told 'em why I no shine flashlight on her: I'm Hawaiian. I'm not supposed to shine nothing on 'em.

So I saw her making that turn going to the other archive building by the state library. I make that turn, she disappear. When I went on the Likelike side, I got a cold, chicken-skin feeling. I walk around about three times looking for her. Gone. I wasn't scared. I'm not supposed to be scared. That's my people. I'm one hundred percent Hawaiian. She's my queen.

I told my superior, my auntie in the palace. I came up and talked to her, talked to *tūtū* lady, and she told me, "Good luck to you."

I told the curator about that, the same story I telling you. He was jumpy, but you know he told me way back one year, so-and-so, somebody before me, saw something—not a woman, a man—same spot, too.

He told me sometimes he's working in his office in the state archives late at night—he stay up there late, about 3 o'clock in the morning—Lili'uokalani talks to him, tell him time for go home.

The second time I saw her was in 1996, right next to her statue. I was working that night on patrol 3 o'clock to 11 o'clock. At the time, they were moving from the capitol tower to the state capitol, and I saw the *wahine* all right. She was dressed in black and carrying something in her hand, I don't know what—flowers, maybe.

She was using the freight elevator, the one going to the *makai* side. The elevator door never opened. Only arrow pointing up. She passed through the door. I asked the workers, "Did you see someone use that elevator?"

"No, that elevator is closed."

I called my sergeant. He asked people if they saw any woman passing by, and they said, "No." Nobody saw her. Only me. He told me go down and drink coffee.

I ask people, the very old people, how come she shows to me two times. Hawaiians got meanings, you know, but they don't know. Sometimes tourists, Japanese and people from the mainland, they see the picture of Kamehameha in the palace. They come out and take my picture. They say I look like him. I don't know. Maybe that's why she appears on me twice. I don't know.

Get plenty stories, plenty before me. Nobody tells 'em. They keep 'em to themselves. Maybe they worry people think they're, you know, *lōlō*. I like come out, tell the truth, tell what I see there. You hold 'em to yourself, no good. Talk to the security guards now, they got plenty of stories.

Ruben Makua, born and raised in Honolulu, served twelve years as the night security guard at 'Iolani Palace. Since 1996, he has worked the day shift as the security guard at Kalihi-Palama Public Library, where he has, so far, seen nothing out the ordinary.

'Iolani Palace

America's only palace, created by King David Kalākaua, who spared no expense on "western symbols of royalty," took four years to build, cost $360,000—and nearly bankrupted the kingdom. An Italian Renaissance design with Corinthian columns, the ten-room palace had electricity before America's White House and a direct phone line to the king's Royal Boat House.

Cherished by latter-day royalists, the 1882 palace stands as a flamboyant architectural statement of the monarchy period, a symbol of the last days of kings at the height of their power.

In the reign of Queen Lili'uokalani, the Kingdom of Hawai'i fell in a January 17, 1893, palace coup led by U.S. Marines at the demand of sugar planters and missionary descendants. Hawai'i's last queen became a prisoner in her own royal house.

A woman resembling Queen Lili'uokalani is often sighted in the royal bedchamber on the second floor or wandering the grounds of 'Iolani Palace after dark, according to security guards and others who work at night in the vicinity.

I always thought of Camp Erdman and Kaimukī Library as warm, happy, safe places. Then I heard about the cats. One is white, the other is black, and neither one is really alive. Or are they? You can decide for yourself after reading Crystal Tamayose's "Camp Erdman's Haunted Cabin" and Alexis Cheong Linder's "The Halloween Cat of Kaimukī." In either place, I'd be careful.

Camp Erdman's Haunted Cabin

On September 30, 1997, I went on a trip with friends to Camp Erdman. On that same day we went hiking to the North Shore. One of my friends found bones of some sort in the sand and brought them back to our cabin (number 24).

After we got back, she asked somebody about the bones, and they said they could be some animal's bones or possibly a child's.

After they said that she freaked out and had some friends help her bury them right in the back of Cabin 24.

That night we were all getting ready to go to bed, but my friend was too scared to go to sleep, so she stayed up.

One of her friends stayed up with her. They were looking out the window, and my friend saw a pure white kitten staring at her with red eyes.

"Omigod, omigod, omigod," she screamed.

"What? What's wrong?" her friend asked.

"There's a pure white cat out the window."

Her friend looked but couldn't see a thing.

"It's right there," she said.

Then the cat started to fade away—and it was gone. Then the air started to get icy cold, then warm again, and she realized it was the kitten that haunts Cabin 24.

Crystal Tamayose is a twelve-year-old student at Kaimukī Intermediate on Oʻahu. She has an older sister and a younger brother and likes to shop, talk on the phone, ride her bike, and spend time with friends.

The Halloween Cat of Kaimukī

Shelly always decorated her desk for Halloween. Bats, sinister teddy bears, a witch's hat, jack-o'-lanterns, and a mechanical black cat with an arching back put us all in the holiday spirit. We liked the black cat best of all. It had a motion detector in it, so every time someone walked by, it gave off a creepy, high-pitched "meow." Some of us played with it so much that the constant "meowing" got on other people's nerves. To accommodate those who hated that mewing cat, Shelly would turn off the motion detector. But after a while, someone else would always turn it back on. Finally, she removed the batteries. The cat perched silently on her desk, waiting and watching for Halloween.

• • •

It had been a quiet Halloween night at the library. No one played any mean pranks like setting the bookdrop on fire or dumping soda in it. By 7:45 the library was pretty empty. We figured that most people were out trick-or-treating or attending a party.

At 8 o'clock we eagerly secured the library, checking the bathroom and between the rows of books, making sure we didn't lock anyone inside. No one wanted to return to the dark library to let a patron out, especially on

Halloween night.

Rose and I were the last to leave. We lingered at the open back door discussing the day's events in the glow of the loading dock lights. Then we heard a faint noise in the workroom. It sounded as if someone was clearing their throat. We stopped talking: our ears tried to tune into the strange sounds drifting out of the dark workroom. We heard soft shuffling, footsteps, and then a distinct "meow" coming from the cat on Shelly's desk.

"Whoa, what was that?" Rose looked at me. Her eyes were wide with disbelief. "Didn't Shelly remove the batteries from that thing?"

Nodding slowly, I stared at her. "Rose," I squeaked, "let's get the hell out of here." We slammed the door behind us, shutting in whatever it was that made the black cat with no batteries "meow."

I started my car and began backing out. But I couldn't resist one last look at the back door. The lights had gone out! "And you stay here, don't follow us home!" I yelled in the direction of the back door. Rose and I sped through the parking lot and out the driveway. I hoped that whatever was in the library would be gone by the next day.

• • •

When we told our coworkers what happened to us, they just laughed and called us a couple of scaredy cats. But later on, Randy took me aside and whispered, "Did you know that the printer by the men's bathroom will start printing all by itself, even when it's off?"

"Does it print anything?" I asked. "I mean, it has a full ink cartridge, right?"

"Yeah, it moves across the page, but it doesn't print anything at all! But don't say anything, okay? I don't want people to get freaked out." With that comment, she walked away. I guess whatever was in the Kaimukī Library is still there after all.

Alexis Cheong Linder has been the young adult librarian at the Kaimukī Public Library for the past five years. She grew up in the *ahupuaʻa* of Koʻolaupoko and Kona on the island of Oʻahu. Her current research topic is a transcultural comparative analysis of the origins of pickled pigs feet.

Hawai'i welcomed the young California couple with open arms in the late '70s. Their first two years were filled with making their new Olomana house, in the hills above Kailua on O'ahu's windward side, a home. They worked on the successful development of their small remodeling business and supported their young son as he found his place at Maunawili Elementary School. They considered their move to Hawai'i a good one, and found that their normal flow of good luck and good times seemed to flourish in their new home. And then the flow shifted at . . .

Hale o Olomana

We were lying in bed reading late one evening when the first evidence of the shift was felt, literally. Jerry was distracted from his book by a gradual awareness of pressure on the lower part of his legs. He became conscious of an invisible presence sitting there, holding his legs firmly to the bed. Fearful and uncomfortable, in his "handle the situation" way he told the presence to leave.

Immediately afterward, he found the event hard to reconcile with his "Archie Bunker" attitude that spirit stuff is fluff, yet the episode was so real to him he had to admit that it really did happen. He took a deep breath and told Debby what happened. As she listened, she knew something must be giving them a message.

And so we began an examination of recent events in our lives. Were they somehow related to this "visit"? Debby had been in a serious accident, totaling her car, and the neighbor's toddler had tragically drowned in their pool. There was also an underlying, hard-to-define sense of imbalance and lack of control, and a feeling that the walls of the house had become cold. We were no longer enjoying the warm, welcoming home we cherish. The good luck and good times were not rolling so easily, and a general sense of dissatisfaction settled upon us.

We began to wonder whether the stories we were hearing about the spirituality of Mt. Olomana, the tri-peaked mountain that rose nearly out of our backyard, might have a bearing upon our experiences. We were told of spirits, unsettled and unready to move into the afterlife, who, in their confusion, played pranksterlike tricks on the current inhabitants at the base of their mountain. Were we now subjects of these tricksters? Had we somehow gotten in their way? Was it time to have our house blessed, as we had heard was the custom? We asked these questions of ourselves as we went on with our busy lives, but with a continuing sense of unrest.

• • •

As happens when we underestimate the lessons presented to us, the message was made clear in the middle of one gruesome night. We were awakened by the sounds of crunching and snapping directly outside our bedroom window. At first we thought it was just 'Ele 'Ele Nani, our trusty black lab, chewing on a bone or a ball or whatever else she might have found. But something about the persistence of the sound prompted Jerry to go outside and investigate. He was surprised to see a large brindle pit bull standing under our window. The powerful dog met his gaze with deep yellow eyes as it slowly backed across the yard and out through the open gate. This was disconcerting, since dogs do not typically hold eye contact with humans. It also seemed strange that the gate was wide open, since our wood shop was in the carport and we were quite careful about closing the gate at night. 'Ele 'Ele Nani watched the drama with her usual calm acceptance; she was a gentle dog, but it seemed odd that she would have let this strange dog into the yard.

Jerry was shaken, with a churning of primal fear in his stomach. But curious as to what the dog had been chewing, he returned to the area of the yard outside the window. Another shock met him head on: he found the remains of our son's two pet rabbits. Their cage had been ripped apart by the pit bull.

Though telling our son, Walker, that his rabbits were dead was difficult, it was even more difficult to face the possibility that we really might need some help dealing with the events being presented to us. We called a Hawaiian friend who we knew was connected to a *kāhuna* lineage. She agreed to call her aunty, who performed blessings. After hearing only a few words about the spiritual visitations, Aunty asked, "Have the spirits yet sat on their legs?" She advised us, through our friend, to deal with the situation immediately, since next the spirit would sit on the chest or face, causing a suffocating feeling.

She offered to bless our house in such a way that the spirits would no longer be able to move through our space. We were reluctant to have this type of exorcism, since we wanted to share our home, not keep anyone, human or spirit, from passing through. We have always felt, especially in Hawai'i, that we are visitors upon this land, with no rights to exclusivity.

Jerry decided he would climb Mt. Olomana and meet whatever needed to be met. In doing this, he was grappling with his skeptic's role, relaxing his practical belief system enough to accept the possibility of the unknown. He was nervous about this change, but little did he know the test to which he was to be put.

• • •

As a family we had all played on Olomana Peak and hiked other local trails. We had learned to leave a blessing of ti leaf and stone to show reverence to the beauty and peace surrounding and within us. Early in the morning, Jerry picked ti from our backyard, under our bedroom window. As the sky began to brighten in the east, he and 'Ele 'Ele Nani headed out across the well-worn path through the pastures leading to the mountain trail. They followed the fence line, moving with surety along the often-trekked trail.

Suddenly, Jerry found himself disoriented. He was no longer near the fence, and he wasn't where the trail started up the mountain ridge. He climbed a tree to see if he could get his bearings and found that he was nearly a quarter mile from the fence line. He climbed down and crossed to where he was able to pick up the mountain trail as it headed over the saddle to the ridge line.

As he headed up the hill, he stopped to collect rocks to add to his ti leaves as blessings. He chose a rock for each member of his family: one for Debby, one for Walker, and last, one for himself. As he placed his rocks in the backpack, he was suddenly weighed down by what seemed a hundred pounds.

This was almost too much for him to bear. He thought perhaps he was losing his mind. He took deep breaths and realized that even if it was all in his mind he needed to continue, to persevere through the challenges presented.

The sun rose majestically as he made his way up the narrow ridge of Olomana with his gift of ti and stone for the house and each member of his family. Morning bloomed. He reached the point of the trail where the other peaks of the mountain come into view, a place he had been many times. This morning those peaks rose up in a new splendor, revealing a power he had never before felt. As he gazed with a startled vision at the mountain, the wind became more than wind; he felt a touch upon his cheeks that could only be described as spiritual and intended.

His fear became more intense, accompanied by a determination to follow the path to its end. The next challenge, physical this time, took place where the path becomes a perpendicular cliff with cables to assist climbers to the next level. At this point he told 'Ele 'Ele Nani to stay below, and with a fear he had never before felt at the cables, and a determination beyond any he had ever known, he bested the perpendicular and shakily made it to the top of the peak. He emptied his backpack of a water bottle, an orange, three rocks, and three ti leaves. Looking out across the early morning light bathing Kailua and its bay, he felt a great sense of accomplishment and wondered whether this really was a trial or insanity.

But finish he must, so he picked up Walker's rock, rolled it up in the ti leaf, and knotted the stem. As he held it in his hands, he saw Walker playing in his room with friends. Sunlight was pouring in all the windows, making the room a warm and inviting cocoon.

After placing Walker's blessing in a safe crevice, he wrapped ti around the rock for Debby. He then envisioned her standing at our front door in a *holokū* gown, welcoming guests into their home. Sunlight poured in the front door, with Debby standing in its rays. As gatekeeper, she held the power to bring in the light. He found a spot for her blessing and placed it tenderly.

Wrapping his own rock, Jerry tried to see himself in their home, but the vision changed. He found himself in the ocean, held by the ocean, as by a mother's arms. Having spent most of his life in or on the ocean, he was suffused by a feeling of comfort and safety. So he placed his blessing with his family's and was ready for the descent. The trip down the mountain was unencumbered. He met 'Ele 'Ele Nani waiting for him below the cables, and they romped their way down, relishing the freedom of a challenge well met.

● ● ●

While Jerry was on his trek, Debby, nervous about their ordeal, decided to take a walk. Passing a house on one of the streets in the neighborhood, she saw a pit bull tied in a carport. Not having seen the dog when he so violently visited their yard, she hesitated to confront the owners until Jerry could identify it. Upon Jerry's return, they walked down the street to the house. The dog was not there. The owners said there had never been a pit bull tied in their carport.

Walker came home from school in the afternoon. Upon entering the house, he commented that it felt brighter and more open, and that the walls felt warmer. In the following weeks, friends asked if we had painted, rearranged furniture, put up new pictures. No, we had not, but the warmth of our home had returned along with the flow of good luck and good times. We had learned a new respect for the possible powers that feed the flow.

Debby and Jerry now live on and caretake a *kama'āina* estate on O'ahu's north shore. They still own their Olomana house. Their son, Walker, is a musician and music teacher in Ashland, Oregon. One of Hawai'i's finest woodturners, Jerry creates one-of-a-kind bowls sought after by collectors and corporations. An avid mountain biker, he has circumnavigated O'ahu and the Big Island of Hawai'i on two wheels. He works with Hawai'i Wildlife Foundation on Kure Atoll, Laysan, and Midway to increase the endangered monk seal population. He is a member of the Pacific Handcrafters Guild, the American Association of Woodturners, and of course, Ko'olau Peddlers.

Debby Kermode is Jerry's partner in business and in life. She says, "Jerry turns the bowls and I do everything else." Debby volunteers as president of The Alliance for Drama Education, a not-for-profit organization promoting drama education as a "rehearsal for life." Debby has been a member of Hālau 'O Ku'ulei Aloha for fourteen years. She helped with the monk seals on Kure Atoll. She does not mountain bike.

Since the early '80s I have lived at the beach in Lanikai on O'ahu's windward side, which enjoys one of the most agreeable, comfortable climates in the world. But, once or twice each year, the day holds its breath and the sun seems way too hot. Even people accustomed to living in the tropics complain. Everyone gets "dat burning feeling back of da eah." In Jeff Gere's story, it's not just the heat that's intense . . .

When Kona Winds Blow

Nobody had a story for me after my performance for seniors at Kailua Park. Darn. Unlocking my car door, I heard my name called hoarsely. A gaunt old Hawaiian man hurried toward me, wheezing and waving his hands.

"Oh, Mr. Gere, I SO enjoyed your talk, OH."

We shook hands. I mumbled something. His cloudy eyes gleamed, and he had a long turkey neck.

"I just HAD to come after you. SURE you're a busy guy, but betcha have a minute for a story. Yep, well PER-HAPS you know my SON? He's a VERY famous *kumu hula* here, Johnny Kalaniana'olealoha'āinaonaumaka . . . [on and on]."

"No, sorry, I don't."

"FAMOUS!" . . . teaches the *keiki* an' *tūtū*, *kahiko* an' *'auwana*, EVERY-thing . . . goes to the Merrie Monarch an' all . . . his specialty is doing traditional chants that are new."

Curious. "How's that work?" I asked.

"Well, that's my story.

"He was raised here in Kailua by my father and grand-father while my wife and I were working. My grandfather built the house. OH! what a view of Kāne'ohe Bay! Now the mountainside is kinda STEEP, see, so he built a rock wall foundation and the two-story house on top of that.

OH! you MUST come visit! Now they BOTH spoke Hawaiian to the boy—the OLD Hawaiian. You don't hear that too much anymore. So he grew up bilingual, see? Now he and HIS family have the house.

Well, one day we were cleaning up in the basement. I was taking a box of junk out the double doors that face Kona and I happened to look up. Above the door and on the side with the rock bench the ceiling was burned black! I turned an' said, 'Son, it's NO GOOD lighting a fire under the HOUSE!' HEH! It's a joke, see, because the roof of the basement is the floor of the HOUSE, see. I gotta chuckle outta that.

But my son looked up at me alarmed. 'What, Daddy, I nevah tell you?'

'Tell me WHAT, son?'

'Oh, Daddy. Daddy, sit down.'

He rubbed his chin a minute. 'A couple of times a yeah, when da Kona winds blow, I get dis burning feeling behind my eah, an' I know she coming. I put da kids an' wife in bed an' move all da fans down heah—da little ones in a circle, da tall ones wid da stands behind dat. Den I wait . . . . I wait, 'cuz I know Madam Pele gonna come an' visit me. 'Ae, Daddy, Pele. Firs' come da *oli* on da wind wit' tales of long ago—I wen chant 'em all so many times . . . . An' me, I ansah wid praise fo' Pele. Den I turn on da fans, 'cuz I know is gonna get hot. She come in dat doah an sit wheah you stay, an' fo' maybe fifteen minute she chant to me, *kahiko*, say what she been doin' an' tin-kin'. Dis fo' real, Daddy. I cannot believe I never tell you.'

'PELE? The fire goddess PELE?! This is fantastic! OH! But tell me: what does she LOOK like?'

'She big . . . maybe six foot seven, six foot eight . . . big bones, no fat . . . big ahms, big nose . . . deep brown skin, long black haiah flow wild down da back . . . and da eyes, Daddy, HER EYES! When she staht to chant, it staht getting hot, REAL hot, Daddy! Her eyes staht to glow red! Dull at firs', den hotter and brighter, like get one dimmah switch! Bright, den dull, up an' down. Big voice too! Ho, she shake da house! An' as she get into it, I stay heatin' up. Firs' my eyebrows an' da haiah on my ahm staht to wilt an' crinkle, like one dry leaf. Den come da sweat. I talking BUCKETS, Daddy! Sweatin' so much get one pool by my feet! One time I see green stuff—like pus—running off my fingahs! An' I squintin', 'cuz da *oli* stay burning me. Is like she reach right into my head, Daddy. Intense! Intense. I concentrate all I got on da *oli* 'cuz if I wen' lose 'em an' freak in da heat, I be flame an' go up like one match.'

He snapped his fingers. *'Pau!'*

He paused. 'Dat few minute seem like houahs.' He paused again. 'I tink she come 'cuz I undahstan' an' 'cuz I can take da heat. When she go I chant my *aloha* to her. An' every time, soon as she go, I fall down righ' in da middle o' da fans an' da goo. I mean, I done used up, spent already . . . every time.

'An every time, at dawn when da birds firs' burs' into song, me, I wake up. HO, I tell you! I wake up ALIVE, Daddy, really ALIVE! I giddy an' happy all ovah like one little kid! Is like I nevah seen cullahs befoah, like I nevah see my own house! I NEW! Every time! I rush upstaiahs quick to scribble da words o' da *oli*—scribble fas' 'cuz da chant is going off in my head! Oh, it come t'rough me clean, like rain outta da sky. An' I can see inside o' me how da hula gonna be, Daddy! Take sometime maybe two years fo' da *halau* to get 'um jes right. Gotta be PERFEC'! Den I show 'um. So dats why da ceiling stay black. Is 'cuz o' what happen wen da Kona winds blow an' I get dat burning feeling back of my eah.'"

He went away and I slumped in my car. The power of his tale settled into me and I started to cry. "My god! I've just heard how a prehistoric goddess continues to update her life story through a man living here, today, like I do. I'm so lucky I live Hawai'i. So, so lucky."

Jeff Gere is a master storyteller and puppeteer who has electrified audiences of all ages throughout Hawai'i and the mainland for over a decade, performing at schools, museums, prisons, homeless shelters, community centers, retreats, conferences, festivals, and conventions. As the Drama Specialist for the Department of Parks and Recreation since 1987, Jeff created and directs the Bankoh Talk Story Festival, Hawai'i's largest celebration of storytelling and oral history.

Pele's Chair

I always wondered what that giant throne-like stone was out there. Not until I read Van James's *Ancient Sites of Oʻahu* did I learn that the lava rock outcropping once was a resting spot for Madame Pele and that many Hawaiians still call it Pele's Chair.

It is said that Madame Pele herself sat here before departing Oʻahu for the Big Island to continue her work at Kīlauea Volcano. In 1826, a New England missionary described a "pagan image" resembling the chair, which he tried to destroy, but Pele's Chair survives to this day. The missionary's fate remains unknown, but I bet Madame Pele knows.

Dogs and cats have a keen
sense of smell. They "see"
things we don't. My cat, Lōlō,
sees aliens in broad daylight
behind every door. I know by
their barking which nights my
neighbors' dogs sense night
marchers. Many people have
told me about their
pets avoiding certain places
on Oʻahu and other islands.
I wanted to believe them, but
I thought strange encounters
by animals difficult to prove.
Until I heard about
the cat and . . .

The Stinky Ghost

About four years ago, a friend of mine, Hinano, moved into the lower floor of the two-story house I share with my husband and my son. It was to be only for a short while; she had a cat and was having difficulty finding a place to rent. A few days after she moved in, a large white outdoor cat began throwing itself into Hinano's glass lanai door. It would hit the glass, shake its head, and repeat the process all over again. We all thought it was because Luke, Hinano's cat, was sitting on the other side of the glass door and taunting the poor thing. Later that evening, though, we noticed a strange odor in Hinano's dining room, and then later in her bedroom. It smelled like wet dirt and tobacco. Luke was staring at the ceiling and going crazy.

Several nights later, the large white outdoor cat again threw itself into the lanai door over and over. Joking, I said, "Well, maybe it's seeing a spirit walking through the door and is just trying to follow it!" We all laughed—until we smelled the wet dirt and tobacco and Luke went nuts again.

Two weeks later, a young girl from Guam came to stay with us for the summer. Since she was enrolled in Mid-Pacific Institute's chamber music program, I rented a piano for her. The piano was right next to the kitchen door, so every night Hinano made sure the piano bench was pushed in so no one would run into it on the way to the kitchen. Every morning, not only was the piano bench away from the piano, but the legs had dented the carpet as if a very heavy person had been sitting on the bench. And there was that smell. Wet dirt and tobacco.

At this point, we concluded that we had one stinky ghost on our hands, and we politely asked it to please take a bath!

I noticed that the more kids there were in the house, the more often the ghost came around. Sometimes it would come upstairs, and the smell would be in my son's room.

One time after my son and I had a terrible fight, I was sitting on the lanai looking out at my view from atop 'Ālewa Heights, feeling quite sorry for myself, when I thought I heard my son come into the room to apologize to me. Instead, I saw a large older man wearing a gaudy vintage Hawaiian shirt. I knew instantly it was our ghost. I had the feeling that he knew I was hurting and had come to comfort me. He still needed a bath.

One time I was practicing the piano downstairs and I smelled the sickly odor and felt air wafting around my legs, down by the pedals. I jumped up from the piano, very scared, and yelled, "Okay, you are welcome to play the piano, but not when I'm playing it!"

My young friend went back to Guam, Hinano and Luke moved to the mainland, and I very rarely smell my friendly ghost anymore. But interestingly, one evening I was at a party up on Pacific Heights and got to talking to the wife of a friend of mine from Rotary. When I said I lived on the next ridge over, with a view similar to the one from this house, she said she used to live in 'Ālewa Heights, on Kaumailuna Place—the street where I live now. She had lived in the house across the street from mine thirty-three years ago! I had to ask her: did she know who lived in my house then? She said yes—in fact, her children used to play in the yard. A widow lived there, and the yard was filled with plumeria trees.

I joked that the husband may have died, but that he hadn't ever left the house. That's when she turned to me and said, "Oh, that's right. You live in the house with the stinky ghost! My children used to come home and tell me they would see something, and then a smell would come, and the cats in the yard would go crazy."

I was shocked, but also relieved, since my husband had heard her tell the whole story and knew at last that I hadn't made up the story of the stinky ghost.

Andrea and David Bills have lived in Honolulu for twenty years. Andrea has her own showroom as a manufacturer's representative, and David is a civil engineer with Gray Hong Bills and Associates. Andrea's son, Phillip, attends Mid-Pacific Institute. They have lived in the house with the stinky ghost for ten years.

On a postcard-perfect day in Hawai'i, an Air Force veteran visiting his daughter on O'ahu makes a pilgrimage to Honolulu's most famous war memorial, the USS *Arizona*. While reading names carved in stone, he is startled to hear voices of young sailors, voices that can only belong to . . .

Arizona Ghosts

As we left Camp Bellows bound for Pearl Harbor to visit the USS *Arizona* Memorial, it was another of those beautiful days in Hawai'i that attract people from all over the world. My wife, Shirley, and I were in Hawai'i to visit our daughter, who lives on O'ahu. We were filling up the days that she had to be at work by taking in the usual tourist sites.

The trip across the island from the windward side via the Pali Highway was beautiful, the traffic wasn't bad, and we found the parking lot for the memorial without any problems.

The boat ride across the harbor was pleasant, and the view of the memorial as we approached it was impressive. I thought the concept of an open-air structure spanning the sunken ship was a magnificent idea that brought one close to the tragic events of that day.

I was not at all prepared to be so deeply moved as I was by the chapel-like room at the end of the memorial where the names of those who lost their lives on the Arizona were carved into the stone wall. As I was reading some of the names, I began to sense the presence of two sailors between me and the space between the guardrail and the wall where the names are inscribed. I couldn't really see anything, but I knew the sailors were there, and I could almost see their uniforms. I felt the hair on the

back of my neck standing on end, and I wondered if anyone else felt their presence or if I was having some sort of
hallucination. I tried to focus my eyes on them, but there
wasn't anything of substance to focus on; however, I
could hear their voices. In a pleading tone they were asking, "What happened? Where are we?"

A moment later they were joined by a third sailor,
who I felt was trying to communicate directly with me. I
still get goose bumps (what people in Hawai'i call chicken
skin) when I remember the intensity of the imploring look
in his eyes and his melancholy plea, "I want to go home.
Please help me go home." I had the sensation that they
didn't realize they were dead, and couldn't figure out
what had become of them. They were asking for help. I
wanted to reach out to them, to let them know they had
been dead for over fifty years and were free to move on—
but how?

This encounter brought tears to my eyes, and it was all
I could do to keep from sobbing out loud. My feelings
obviously showed, because Shirley asked me if I was upset
because I had known someone on the *Arizona*. I didn't
when we arrived at the memorial, but now there are three
who will be very close to me for the rest of my life, even
if I never learn their names.

Thomas N. Colbath's twenty-three years in the Air Force included eight years
in Germany and a tour in Vietnam. In 1996 he retired after twenty years on
the electronics faculty at Austin (Texas) Community College. Since then, he
has visited Hawai'i twice and hopes to return frequently.

Pearl Harbor

Ghosts are thick as oil that still oozes out of the sunken battleship USS *Arizona*—"a droplet escaping every nine seconds," according to Thurston Clarke, author of *Pearl Harbor Ghosts*.

The hull, an underwater tomb for 1,100 lost sailors and marines killed in the Japanese air raid on December 7, 1941, continues to deteriorate and emit eerie noises.

"You can hear it bubbling and gurgling," Daniel Lenihan, of the National Park Service's Submerged Cultural Resource Unit, told the *Honolulu Star-Bulletin*. "It's making sounds and dripping and bleeding."

Twenty U.S. ships sank that day, but seventeen rose to fight again. The *Oklahoma* was scrapped in 1946; the *Utah*, with fifty-eight sailors, lies underwater on the west side of Ford Island. The *Arizona*, which never fired a shot in combat, became one of the world's most famous war monuments.

The celebrated battleship *Missouri*, upon whose decks the Emperor of Japan surrendered in Tokyo Bay on VJ Day, September 2, 1945, is now anchored triumphantly in Pearl Harbor, an iconic bookend to "the last, great war," as my father, the World War II pilot, and his brave generation called it.

A baby girl in Waimānalo is possessed by a wandering spirit in this chilling story that reveals the mysterious power of Hawaiian *'alaea* and ti leaf in the struggle to save . . .

Lilia

Lilia was born to my cousin, Nohealani, in 1987. She was a beautiful child with a sunny smile and dancing brown eyes. They lived on the homestead in Waimānalo, a small town in windward Oʻahu. It was to this sleepy town that my great-grandfather brought his family to live in 1903 and where members of my family remain to this day.

Lilia brought so much love and aloha to the household. She was the apple of her *tūtū*'s eye and a wonderful blessing to her aunty.

When she was a few months old, Lilia began to cry a lot; nothing anyone did could make her stop. When she was finally quiet, she'd sit up and stare. It was as if something or someone was communicating with her—but there was no one there!

Nohealani became alarmed one day when she found Lilia sitting up in her crib, looking at one spot, and having a conversation with someone or something that wasn't there. She didn't know what to do and called my dad to ask for advice. Dad gave some ti leaves to Nohealani and told her to put one above the door to Lilia's room and one near her crib. Things got better for the next couple of months.

About two weeks prior to her first birthday, it started happening again. Lilia would be sitting in her crib, staring at the same spot, and talking to someone or something—but there was no one there! Nohealani called my dad again and he brought more ti leaves to put in Lilia's room. There were no more disturbances until after Lilia's first birthday celebration.

Lilia's baby luau was so much fun. The 'ohana was there—my brothers even flew in from Chicago. Children were playing outside, the food was 'ono, and the entertainment was wonderful.

Tūtū invited most of us over to the house the next day to eat leftovers. Everyone sat outside in the front yard, eating, playing music, and relaxing. In the late afternoon, after too many beers, my brother, who was sitting under a coconut tree facing the house, began to swear, telling me, "There's an old lady walking through the *laua'e* patch going to the window of Lilia's room." He swore and yelled, "Get out of there!"

I approached my brother and asked him to calm down. He kept saying, "You folks, that lady's going to Lilia's room!" The only thing is, no one else could see the old lady! We all shrugged this incident off, but my brother kept insisting that the old lady was there. We finally took him home to sleep it off.

A few nights later, Nohealani called Dad; she was distressed. Lilia was in her crib screaming. Nothing could stop her. When Nohealani tried to pick her up, it felt as if something or someone was holding the baby down. Try as she might, there was no way she could lift the baby out of the crib. And Lilia had red marks on her arms and legs—as if she were being held down.

Aunty finally got Lilia free. They wrapped her in a blanket and rushed her to the emergency room. By the time they reached the clinic, Lilia was smiling and happy as can be, and all of the red marks had simply disappeared.

There was no explanation to give the doctor, either! Upon returning home, Nohealani called Dad again. He told her he would go to the house the next day and stay in the baby's room to see if he could "feel" anything.

The next day, Dad got sick suddenly and could not go to Waimānalo. He asked my sister and me to go in his place. He gave us 'alaea salt, some ti leaf that he had prepared, and instructions on how to use them.

"First, your minds must be clear of all things; you must concentrate on Lilia. Go outside the house, pray, and throw the salt around the whole house, leaving an opening near the baby's room. You must not be deterred from doing this. If something is there, it will try to make your mind wander so that you cannot complete the task. Keep your mind strong!"

With these words in our thoughts, my sister and I got in the car and drove to Waimānalo. Once we got there, we went upstairs to be with Lilia for a while and then proceeded outside to begin our prayer. My three children sat downstairs under the plumeria tree along with Tūtū and Aunty. My sister held the bowl while I prayed and threw the 'alaea salt.

As we approached Lilia's room, I was stopped dead in my tracks by the sight of a *maunaloa* vine that was covering the avocado tree—it was in full bloom! The tree was completely covered with lavender blossoms. I was breathless at the sight, and I stopped what I was doing. I had lost my concentration—just as Dad had predicted! My sister grabbed my arm and shook me, saying, "Madelyn, you can't stop now!"

At this point, the avocado tree began to shimmer and shake gently and an elderly Hawaiian woman wearing a light blue *mu'umu'u* and a kerchief around her neck came out of the *laua'e* patch.

A dirt path in the *laua'e* led from the neighboring bushes to the window at Lilia's room. I stood in the path, in a cold sweat, all the hair on my body standing up and the back of my neck tingling. The elderly Hawaiian lady was moving toward me, but she didn't have any feet! I don't remember speaking, but my family told me later that I began to cuss and swear. I admonished the woman for coming to bother Lilia, and I told her that she couldn't have her—Lilia belonged in our family, we loved Lilia. She came right up to me. My children ran to me and tried to grab me, but they couldn't get a grip on me. The woman finally retreated into the bushes, and I fell to the ground, exhausted.

My sister, my children, and my cousins all came to my aid—they had heard me yelling, but no one had seen the woman. I laid ti leaves across the path in the *laua'e* and prayed there. The very next day the *laua'e* patch was as thick and green as ever, with no sign that a path had been there the day before. Also, the very next day there was no *maunaloa* vine and there were no flowers on the avocado tree. No *maunaloa* vine has ever grown and bloomed in that area prior to or since this occurrence.

How can we explain this? I don't know. My cousin had a Hawaiian priest come to bless the house and all of us two weeks later; there have been no incidents since. Today, Lilia is a healthy, active, and much loved eleven-year-old.

Madelyn Horner Fern was born and raised on O'ahu. A graduate of the Kamehameha Schools, she is the mother of three grown children and works as Human Resources Manager at the Sheraton Maui Hotel.

The Island of Maui

When I first met Pat Leilani Young in the early 1980s in Honolulu, I was struck by her tacit belief in events and circumstances and encounters that all seemed illogical and preposterous to me. Her stories were just too incredible. "Oh sure," she would say matter-of-factly about this or that strange occurrence as if it really happened. The more we talked, the more I came to see things the way she does— through Hawaiian eyes. Now, years later, I am beginning to understand about . . .

Connections

I recall several nights, when I was a young child, waking up with a tremendous pressure on my chest. It felt as if there was something sitting on me, but there was nothing there. I could hardly breathe. I told my mother, and she took me to the doctor. Certainly I was too young to have heart problems.

The doctor deduced that it was some sort of stress reaction, caused perhaps by my vivid imagination. (I often thought I saw monsters in the shadows.)

Years later, when I was doing some research on paranormal occurrences in the Islands, I read about crushing ghosts, spirits that actually sit or lie on people as they sleep.

I also discovered that the Diamond Head area, where our home was, used to have a lot of *heiau* and possibly burial sites. That certainly explained a lot. Now I'm convinced that my experiences were supernatural ones.

• • •

My mother and I once spent a few nights at a low-rise garden hotel in Ka'anapali, Maui—Hotel Ka'anapali, I believe. The main section of the hotel was full, so we were given rooms at the edge of a deserted wing. At least we assumed it was deserted, because part of it was being renovated.

About 2 A.M. our first night there, we were awakened by what we thought was a work crew on the grounds. It sounded like a lot of people tramping about. Then we heard the sound of something being dragged, and finally the sound of digging, as though with a pick and shovel—very annoying.

When I finally dropped into a deep sleep, I experienced the sensation of nearly being sucked out of my body through my forehead. It was really strange. I woke up with a start.

The next morning we complained to the desk about the construction noise. The woman was puzzled; there had been no night work, she said. When we came home and mentioned our experience to an old-timer, he said that we had heard night marchers, spirits of ancient warriors or *ali'i* tramping by. An ancient path probably passed right through the hotel grounds, he said. He added that it was a good thing we didn't open the door or look out the window to check for the source. Since we are part-Hawaiian, we would have been struck dead.

The digging? He said that many have experienced strange things in that area of Maui. Perhaps it was the digging of a grave. We got the chills thinking about it.

And the dream? A spirit may have wanted to occupy my body, he said, and was trying to push my soul out.

We believe, of course, in night marchers. (I think they're the reason my *tūtū* used to want us kids indoors by 7 P.M.)

• • •

They say the veil between the physical and spiritual worlds is thin for Hawaiians. The night my dad died I heard him calling me. (I slept in his bed that night to keep Ma company.) "Pssst, Pat." It was very clear. My son, who was at our apartment, heard his unmistakable snoring. And my mother hears him around the apartment often, his keys rattling, his bureau drawer opening, his closet door closing. Several times she's awoken to find him standing by the bed. "Hi, Ma," he says.

In her dreams, she has gone flying with him to misty places. "Do you know where you're going, Sonny?" she asks in her dream. It's so typical of them.

• • •

I was really close to my grandmother. After she died I felt her comforting presence during times of crisis. Sometimes, a small butterfly flutters around my head when I am in a quiet, natural place or at a *heiau*—I mean really follows me around—and I feel that same warm, comforted feeling. I feel that it's my grandmother, staying close.

A beautiful black moth with patterned wings insists on living in the corner of my mother's room. She tries to chase it out the door, but it always comes back. I feel that it's Dad, staying close. She acts as if she thinks I'm "tetched" in the head, but I think she has an inkling it might be true. As long as you've got Hawaiian blood, you have the connection.

Pat Leilani Young, born in Honolulu, writes a column for the *Honolulu Advertiser.*

Things happen that are
meant to be—
but how and why?
Those are the cosmic questions
Doug Self asks in . . .

Mystery on Maui

In May 1987 my partner, Guy, and I were living in Southern California. Neither of us was entirely satisfied with our lives. Guy was working as an advertising executive and was suffering from stress and burnout. I had just started to make headway in my career as an actor, but I was still unhappy with the type of work I was getting.

Hoping for some kind of change, I picked up Shakti Gawain's *Creative Visualization* and started doing the exercises. I was trying to envision a better life—one that would be both rewarding for Guy and me and beneficial to others. Before long, I began to sense that there was a piece of land in Hawai'i calling to us.

We were to go there and become flower farmers. This was about the wackiest thing I could have come up with, but it did make sense considering our desire for a simpler way of life, where we could grow our own food and enjoy the surf year-round.

A month later, we flew to the islands to look for this mysterious piece of land. I didn't know which island we'd find it on, but through my visualization work, I did know that the land would have five specific attributes: It would measure two acres, be on or near the ocean, in a welcoming neighborhood, and have fertile soil and a good growing climate.

As soon as we landed on Maui, I had the feeling that

this was the right island. But nothing the real estate sales-person showed us seemed right. Then, at the end of the day, he mentioned one last property on the island's north shore. As it turned out, the 2.003-acre property met all our criteria: it was a fertile lot on a high cliff overlooking the ocean, with an exquisite view of Waipiʻo Bay, and it was in a friendly neighborhood. As soon as I walked on the land, I started shaking. My knees got weak, I started sweating, and I knew this was the piece of land that had been calling to us.

When we walked out to the cliff and saw the view, things started to get even more strange. It was as if I could hear the land trying to make a bargain with me. It said if this was to be our land, it could never just be OUR land—we would have to share it. That message came up through my feet from the land, and I said, "Okay, I surrender, I accept. No problem."

We couldn't believe our luck, but when we put in an offer we learned that we were too late. Someone had already put an offer in ahead of us. Devastated, we spent another day looking around, but couldn't find anything we liked.

On our last night in Maui we stayed with a man whose house is just up the road from the property. After telling him how we'd come looking for a special piece of land and that we really thought this was it, he said, "You know, it's really a shame, because I'm sure that Shakti would've loved to sell you guys the land."

"Shakti?" I said, "Shakti who?"

"Shakti Gawain," he replied casually. "You know, the one who wrote the book *Creative Visualization*? She owns that property."

I just about fainted.

But that wasn't the end of it. As it turned out, the

offer ahead of ours had been put in by a man who rented an apartment from our host. Twenty minutes after our host told us about Shakti's connection to the land, the phone rang. Our host went to answer it and soon came back visibly shaken. The call was to tell him that his tenant had just been gunned down in the Bahamas. He was killed as he was leaving his bank, carrying the money for his down payment for the property. He was allegedly a lawyer for arms smugglers, our host went on to say, and apparently some of his enemies had caught up with him. And so we got the land.

It was all very startling—even frightening. For some time afterward I was very nervous about doing any more visualizations, even though somebody getting killed was never a part of my visualization about the land. I talked with Shakti about this, and she told me that I had to realize that I could not have caused the shooting in the Bahamas. That made sense, but it took me a long time to really accept it.

It also took some time before I understood the bargain I had made with the land that first day we saw it. When our flower business couldn't pay the bills, and the bank wouldn't lend us any more money because we didn't have any salaried income, we decided to turn the glassed-in gazebo we'd built near the cliff as a meditation and yoga space into a vacation rental. So it was indeed by sharing the land with others that we were able to stay here—and this also allowed us to bring the special energy of the place to others.

Doug Self, with his partner, Guy Fisher, built and operates Huelo Point Flower Farm on Maui's north shore. Doug's story originally appeared in the May/June 1995 issue of *New Age Journal.*

Sometimes you don't see the signs even when they're in your face. Sometimes you don't know enough to know a sign when you see it. Sometimes, it all begins to make sense. Not that day . . .

In Kahakuloa

Spinner dolphins on Maui's Nākālele Bay. A grinning pit bull at the valley's gate. The rustling pareu on a calm day. The wet rock in the stream that sent me flying. How could I have overlooked all that? Now, years later, I can close my eyes and see the signs for what I think they were: a force in opposition, a wandering spirit, night marchers, the soul of the place. Whatever. Something objected to my presence in the valley that day, and there were signs I failed to heed.

I began to realize this only last September down in the South Pacific, on the island of Huahine, an island with *mana* strong enough to lean on. It happened after the Tahitians found three teeth of their ancestors at the Maeva dig, the day Sinoto fell off the *marae*, the day Michael folded a ti leaf around a rock and we, all three of us, elected without a word not to ascend the Sacred Mountain of Mata'ire'a, where the giant banyan tree once draped with skulls now keeps the *marae* in deep shadow.

That's when I finally came to understand that the supernatural world so easily embraced by Polynesians affects us in different ways. They do not concern themselves with solving riddles. They accept the insoluble. We always want supernatural things to make sense. They are content not to understand. For a long time everything that happened that day in that valley on Maui bothered me because I didn't know that. I do now.

• • •

Kahakuloa Valley lies beyond a locked gate on the far north side of Maui. You may go there now, but only with a guide. The road to the valley is named for Kahekili, The Feather-Caped Thunderer, the king of Maui. Tattooed Marquesan-style over half his body, Kahekili took flying leaps off Pu'u Keka to prove his courage. He built houses out of the skulls of his enemies. Narrow, winding, and rough, the king's road is scary; it edges around sheer sea cliffs without safety rails.

On the way to the valley you pass Kahakuloa, a village so picturesque Gauguin might have painted it: sun-faded houses with red tin roofs on a black sand cove laced with white fishing nets under a green grove of coco palms. I recall a green church with a New England steeple. You want to stay there forever.

Unfortunately, the genuine charm of the village is diminished by the brusque, not very aloha-like scene on the *mauka* side of the road at the gateway to Kahakuloa Valley. The chain link fence is heavily padlocked. It is usually blockaded by jacked-up pickups of young locals who sport tattooed biceps, hang warrior helmets from their rearview mirrors, and consider pit bull dogs with spiked collars a necessary option. Nobody feels welcome here.

• • •

I always wondered why the valley was *kapu* in the contemporary sense and yearned to go there if only to learn the secret of the place. I knew that I must wait to be invited. In Hawai'i, nobody goes willy-nilly into interior valleys, especially one so well defended by locals, without a proper invitation.

One day the invitation did come and from the most unlikely source: John Toner, a blue-eyed blond *haole*, who is The Ritz Carlton Kapalua's general manager and Maui's most unusual host. "Would you like to visit Kahakuloa Valley this weekend?"

"Of course," I said.

An ambassador of cultural exchange, Toner invites Hawaiians to meet guests and sends them out for true encounters. Now, he'd struck a bargain with the residents of the valley so visitors could experience a Hawai'i nearly lost elsewhere in Maui's rush to progress. A day in Kahakuloa Valley was now a Ritz Carlton activity, like snorkeling in Honolua Bay.

"The valley is magical," Toner said. "You'll be delighted."

● ● ●

"I've never seen spinner dolphins," my wife, Marcie, said as we drove the wild coast. As if on cue, Nākālele Bay suddenly exploded with a pod of spinner dolphins, a hundred or more, the most I'd ever seen. Leaping and spinning in tight circles and flipping somersaults, they looked like an aquatic circus gone berserk. We stood on the cliff watching the dolphins so long we almost missed our appointment at the valley gate.

The usual clog of pickup trucks obstructed the entry. In the bed of one truck, I noticed a black pit bull dog because it seemed to be smiling at me, grinning actually, big and wide and friendly. The Cheshire Cat of pit bulls, I thought, and reached for my camera just as two other dogs ran up to meet us. They were followed by a slim, handsome Hawaiian man holding a ring of keys—Oliver Dukelow, our valley guide. A modern Hawaiian who chooses to live an eighteenth-century lifestyle, Dukelow dives for fish, tends his taro patch, and clings to old Hawaiian values that include "respect for my health, my family, the ocean, the mountains, and this valley."

Dukelow inflicts such arcane values on local delinquents with great success; an ex–law enforcement officer, he takes custody of dead-end kids and puts them to work in the valley planting taro, repairing rope bridges, clearing the jungle, and restacking rocks. I realized then that the jam of trucks at the gate probably belonged to his young charges. They leave the valley with a new attitude. Visitors also come away with a new understanding of the culture.

• • •

"Cross the stream, here," he said, pointing to smooth boulders in the fast-rushing stream. "We're working on the bridge." I stepped out upon the biggest rock in the stream, slipped, and went flying into the air. In the fall, I saved my camera from a dunking, but sprained my left thumb and emerged sopping wet, bleeding, and sore, feeling not just clumsy but as if something had deliberately pushed me.

Once I regained my composure and daubed peroxide on my various scrapes, Oliver pointed to his taro patch, told me to kick off my shoes and step into the silky, soft mud. Immediately, I felt a warm sensation spread through my entire body. What's in the mud, I asked, but Oliver laughed and said it was the soul of old Hawai'i. While I stood in soothing primal mud, Dukelow explained how he diverts Kahakuloa Stream into *lo'i*, or taro patches, which he called the cornerstone of Hawai'i's early agriculture.

"Without taro we Hawaiians would wither away—taro is our staple."

We sipped iced tea outside his tidy handcrafted house by the side of the babbling stream in a tropical oasis of banana, papaya, mango, plum, and coconut trees. Then we set out hiking into the valley carved over eons by the stream that originates as a waterfall on mile-high Puʻu Kukui, the second-wettest spot on earth, whose cloud-wreathed summit early Hawaiians believed was the inter-section between heaven and earth. It all began to sound like a kind of paradise, but I knew better, that life here long ago was harsh and brutal and savage. Skulls were crushed because of an errant glance.

The valley, Dukelow said, is full of ancient, mysterious attractions: *heiau*, shrines, platforms, and night marchers—spirits of ancient *aliʻi* who stroll with alacrity through the valley, revisiting lifetime haunts. As we walked alongside chest-high ferns on the banks of the stream, we came upon a white, wood-frame house appar-ently abandoned. "What happened here?" I asked.

"Night marchers," Oliver said, as if he'd seen them himself last night.

The house, he said, sits in the path of night marchers, and he told the story of the former occupant—"that old coconut head"—who against all advice built his house on the night marcher trail. He'd lost his job, his wife, every-thing, Oliver said, because he built his house in the wrong place.

I didn't know whether to believe him and looked to see if he was joking—he wasn't. As we walked by the house I thought I saw a pareu rustling in an open window of the empty house, like they do when trade winds blow, but there had not been a breath of air in the valley all day.

We hiked on deeper into the dead-end valley toward

the waterfall pool, but dense jungle that had never known a machete stopped us. We turned back to follow a foot-path on the east side of the valley, now in full shade. Soon we came upon hard evidence of early inhabitants: terraces and *heiau* and strange C-shaped rock shelters all built, Oliver said, more than 1,500 years ago, centuries before the arrival in Hawai'i of Captain James Cook.

It was deathly quiet here. I felt like Stone Age man in some big city's natural history museum. I shivered in the heat of the day and was glad to leave the shadowy site.

Sitting in full sunlight outside Oliver's house by the babbling stream, "talking story," savoring the moment, I enjoyed a great sense of calm and well-being and wished everyone could experience a Hawai'i like this. It was hard to leave this old Hawaiian place, and I understood the dilemma of the departed and why they return. I thought of the night marchers again when my photographs came back. Only one image came out: the house of the night marchers. The pictures of Oliver and his house, the taro pond and stream, the essence of the valley, all were blank, and I was puzzled. What on earth was going on here? I called Oliver at the number in Lahaina he gave me but he was gone. I told the woman who answered about the pic-tures, how only one came out, and she said she would tell Oliver but he probably already knew. The valley was full of enigmas I would never understand.

• • •

Last September, I joined the famed archaeologist Dr. Yosihiko Sinoto on Huahine for another dig in the pre-historic village of Maeva. Diggers unearthed three human teeth that day. "Tupa pau," the Tahitians said—their word for phantom or ghost. Everyone laughed. Later that day

Dr. Sinoto, his assistant, Michael Pfeffer, and I went up
the Sacred Mountain of Mata'ire'a to measure the stone
walls of a *marae.* I heard a crashing sound, and turned to
see Dr. Sinoto tumble head over heels into sticker weeds.
"I'm okay," he said. Michael wrapped a stone in a ti leaf
and we went back down the mountain. We never said a
word about our sudden departure; it just seemed like a
good idea not to press on. I began to suspect then that
powers beyond our control may and often do appear
when you encounter the soul of a place.

In Kahakuloa, though, I couldn't read the mixed
signals so quickly. The clues, if they were clues, were
ambiguous, conflicting, unclear: spinner dolphins, the
slippery rock, the grinning pit bull, the soothing mud, the
rustling pareu, the sudden chill at the strange C-shaped
structure, my sense of well-being in the sun, the missing
photographs. Signs of approach and avoidance. I felt wel-
come/uneasy. I wanted to stay/flee. Maybe it was all only
my imagination, a coincidence, a prank of nature. I didn't
understand what was going on that day and I probably
never will. What I know is this: I am content not to understand.

Rick Carroll is the author of *Hawai'i's Best Spooky Tales* and *Chicken Skin:
True Spooky Stories of Hawai'i.*

Ever wonder why the lights go out? In this eerie story from Maui, Ben Lowenthal tells the true story of what happened on old Hāna Highway in the 1950s, to a Ha'ikū man everyone once knew as . .

The Lantern Lighter of Māliko Gulch

Māliko Gulch is a deep canyon located between Ho'okipa Park and Ha'ikū. It is known to have been the home of ancient Hawaiians. A *heiau* and the ruins of an ancient village can still be located way in the back of the gulch. Until the 1960s, the bridge on the old Hāna Highway at Māliko was illuminated by lanterns.

In the 1950s, there was a lantern lighter who lived up in Ha'ikū. His job was to walk down the road at dusk and light the lanterns on the bridge.

One dark evening, when the sky was black with clouds blowing in from Hāna-side, the lighter walked down the road to do his job. He lit the lantern on the Hāna end of the bridge and had begun to turn around when—phffft— the lantern went out. There was no wind. Not even a breath of a trade wind breeze. There was nothing. Yet the light went out as if someone blew it out.

The night got blacker, black as the bottom of a pond. The lighter turned around to light the lantern again. As he flicked his match, he saw a face inside the lantern, grinning.

Terror gripped his throat like an icy hand. He slowly relit the lantern, turned quickly, and ran back up the hill to his home. From that day on, he never returned to his job as the lantern lighter and nobody took his place.

A lifelong resident of Banana Patch, Peahi, Maui, Ben Lowenthal is currently a senior at Baldwin High School. He is editor-in-chief of the *Baldwin Courier*, and his interests include Polynesian anthropology and folklore, skateboarding, guitar, and collecting and presenting local ghost stories.

The Island of Kaua'i

Filipinos believe that if you
wiggle your toes,
ghosts will go away.
But they may not stay away,
just like . . .

The Ghost Who Came Back

When Mrs. Bukoski was four years old, her mother died. Ten years later, one night when she was in bed, she felt she wasn't alone. A little alarmed, she looked over her shoulder and saw the darkest thing she ever saw. It was darker than the night's darkness. She was really scared now. But then, with a shaking feeling, she wiggled her toes and the thing vanished.

The next day, Mrs. Bukoski had a spiritual feeling that she had to light a candle for her mother at church, so she did.

The next time the ghost came was on a cool night when Mrs. Bukoski was in college. She was sound asleep in her dorm when she woke up to the feeling that she wasn't alone. She looked at one side of the bed and then the other, and looked back and saw the dark figure she saw many years ago. She squeezed her toes. And it was gone. The next day she went to church and lit a candle. Then she went to her mother's grave and put flowers there. The ghost never came again. But maybe . . .

Aaron Teves is thirteen years old. He is in ninth grade at Kaua'i High and Intermediate School. He is a member of the U.S. Naval Sea Cadet Corps, PMRF Division, and enjoys computers, swimming, and playing pool.

When a mysterious phantom appears in a young girl's room on a hot summer night on the island of Kaua'i, she tries to scream for help but can't. Next morning she learns her night visitor may have been . . .

Great-grandpa

One dark, hot night I couldn't sleep. I moved all over the bed to find a comfortable spot. I turned toward the door and opened my eyes slowly and saw a man or "thing" with shiny glasses. I could only see its face, and its body was unclear. I was so scared; I didn't move a muscle. I even tried not to breathe hard. My heart was beating fast. I tried to yell, "Mom," but it couldn't come out. I just had to do it, so I yelled, "Mom!" as loud as I could. I yelled once more, and my mom came running into my room. When she did, the man or thing was gone. I told my mom what happened, and she left the light on for the rest of the night.

The next morning I told my grandma and grandpa what happened. They asked a lot of questions. Afterwards, they told me that the man was my grandpa's dad. I hope that will never happen again!

Thirteen-year-old Amanda Fahselt is a student at Kaua'i High and Intermediate School. Her hobbies are volleyball and basketball.

On the island of Kaua'i there are ordinary rocks and sacred rocks. Sometimes the two get mixed together and that causes *pilikia*. When a young girl's father uses Po'ipū rocks to build a Kalāheo wall, strange things begin to happen as we learn in . . .

Dad's Encounters

My father was building a moss rock wall in Kalāheo, Kaua'i. He removed the rocks from the Po'ipū area. By the time the wall was finally built, he had removed a lot of rocks without knowing that the area where he found the rocks was a Hawaiian *heiau*, a sacred place.

During this time, at night, while my dad was sleeping, a big, black image came out of the closet and pounced on my dad and held him down. He tried to get him off, but the dark thing, which resembled a big, Hawaiian warrior, kept holding him down. During the struggle, my dad kept shouting, "Get off me!"

My mom, who was in the living room, heard his shouts. She rushed to the room. When she got there, she could see my dad struggling as if he was trying to get somebody off of him.

These encounters went on for several more nights, until my dad spoke with a friend about them. When the friend came to our house, he asked my dad about the rocks my dad was using for the wall. My dad told him they were taken from the Po'ipū area and that the area looks like a *heiau*.

My dad's friend told my dad to plant ti leaves around the four corners of the house and take an offering to the *heiau*. He took an orange and one manju and placed them on the rocks of the *heiau*. He also said "Thank you" for the rocks. After he placed the offering and planted the ti leaves around the four corners of the house, there were no more encounters with the warrior.

Another encounter my dad had occurred while he was working for the Līhuʻe Plantation as a cane haul truck driver. One night my dad headed toward Moloaʻa to pick up a load of cane. While approaching the Wailua Golf Course, he felt a big slap on the right side of his head. Both windows of the truck were rolled up, and nobody was with him at the time. No traffic was visible. The hair on his head stood up as if he saw a ghost. My dad looked around the cab to see if anything had fallen that could have caused the severe blow to his head. The only thing that was hanging in the cab was his jacket, and it had not fallen.

When my dad got back to the unloading station in Līhuʻe, he told some of his fellow workers about the encounter. They told my dad that he probably drove in the area where the night marchers were crossing the road.

My dad had still another encounter while picking ʻopihi at Ahukini on Kauaʻi. My dad heard his name being called out: "Johnny . . . Johnny . . . Johnny . . . ." He looked around, but he saw no one. So he kept on picking ʻopihi, and while unloading his bag of ʻopihi on a rock, he heard his name being called out again. He looked around and still he didn't see anyone. He continued to pick up more ʻopihi, and once again his name was called out as if the voice was coming from the ocean. The first time his name was called, the voice came from far away, toward the area where he parked his car. As soon as he heard his name being called from the direction of the ocean, he packed up and went to my grandpa's house.

My dad told my grandpa what had happened. My grandpa told my dad that he did the right thing by leaving, because if he had answered whoever was calling him, he probably would have never been found.

Chandelle Rego-Koerte, a thirteen-year-old student at Kaua'i High and Intermediate School, likes to swim, talk on the phone, and shop.

In the bookish hush of Hanapēpē library on the island of Kaua'i, a librarian working alone at his desk feels somebody watching him. When he looks up, no one, of course, is there. It is only his imagination. Or is it? At home a few days later, he gets that same feeling, looks up and meets . . .

The Holoholo Man

Never in my life did I encounter a "hair-raising" experience until the past year. I work at the library in Hanapēpē, on the island of Kaua'i. It is a small library with a nice, homey atmosphere. On several occasions, when I sat at my desk, doing some paperwork, I would feel as if somebody was watching me. I'd look up suddenly, but no one was there.

I thought nothing of it until one evening when I was at home working on my computer. Suddenly I felt that someone was watching me again. I looked up and saw the massive body of a man wearing an aloha shirt, standing about three feet away from me. I did not see any head, and I was afraid to look to see if he had any feet.

I could feel the hair on my head rising, and I was so frightened that I felt chicken skin all over my body. I told the man to leave me alone. I quickly turned off the computer and the lights in the room and went to my bedroom.

Several days later, I bought some Hawaiian food for dinner—*laulau, poi,* and *lomi lomi* salmon—and set a plate on the clothes dryer next to my computer. I went into the living room briefly, and when I went back to get the plate I left on the clothes dryer, to my amazement the plate was gone. I was puzzled because I had left it there only a few minutes ago.

I asked my son if he had seen the plate. He said he had, and, in fact, he thought it was one of the children's plates that they left behind and he ate the food. I felt relieved, knowing that the plate did not "disappear" suddenly.

Months went by and then one day I happened to tell a friend of mine about seeing the big Hawaiian man at my house. She casually said that it was her deceased husband going *holoholo* (roaming around) and he had followed me home. She then told me: "Don't feed him. Just tell him to go home."

"Don't feed him!" That made me smile and laugh at what I shouldn't have done.

Richard S. Fukushima was born and raised on Kaua'i. He attended the University of Hawai'i and Kaua'i Community College and served in the United States Army and the Hawai'i Army National Guard. He currently works at the Hanapēpē Public Library. A widower, he enjoys golf, bowling, fishing, cooking, quilting, and writing poetry and short articles. His story "Mamoru" appeared in *Hawai'i's Best Spooky Tales: True Local Spine-Tinglers*.

The Island of Molokaʻi

A Molokaʻi Mū Sighting

Olokuʻi

After sunset on Moloka'i's deserted West End, a forlorn place to be, two young women head back to their vacation condo in a rental car, and can't believe their eyes when they see what can only be . . .

A Moloka'i Mū Sighting

Moloka'i is my favorite island, not just because of its physical, rugged beauty, but because it seems to be the most "natural" island, the least spoiled by civilization. A deep spiritual feeling emanates from the land, and there is a sweetness in the smiles of its people.

In April of 1990, I was there for a long weekend with co-workers. We were staying on the west side of the island.

Near the end of our first day there, my friend Rachel and I were sitting on the warm pink sand at Pāpōhaku Beach near the campground. The sun was setting, and we were the only ones on the beach. The light was *melemele*, the air was soft as silk.

We were in a mellow mood, winding down from our hectic daily work pace, rejoicing in being at our favorite spot, and grateful for each other's company.

But we were getting hungry, and we decided it was time to get some grinds. We hopped into the rental car, turned on the headlights, and pulled out of the parking lot onto the lonely stretch of road heading back to Ke Nani Kai, our condo. Before the car could pick up speed, we both noticed something in the center of the road about twenty-five feet ahead. Rachel stopped the car immediately. Not believing what we saw, neither of us spoke a word.

It did not make a move, for maybe twenty to thirty

seconds. Then it turned toward the left side of the road and continued to cross, disappearing down a path into the tall grass on the other side.

Rachel turned to me and said, "What did you see?"

"I saw something about three-and-a-half feet high, standing upright, with brown fur, two long arms, and glaring, gold eyes," I said. I had been reluctant to speak, not knowing if I had had a hallucination or what. So I was relieved when Rachel said she had seen the same thing.

She pulled the car off the road and said she wanted to follow "it." By now, the rest of the day's light had left and it was almost dark.

Without a flashlight, I didn't want to go down the path, but my curiosity was too great. We got out of the car and walked across the road just where "it" had gone, and saw a path of sorts, very narrow, into the waist-high grass.

The path disappeared after about fifteen to twenty feet, so we turned around to leave. There were no visible signs that anything was still there, but the feeling of being watched was unmistakable.

We ran back to the car, started the engine, and sped down the road back to the condo.

The other friend in our party heard us come in, and upon seeing our faces, said, "What happened? You're both white as sheets!"

Now for *haole* Rachel, that's not a surprising description, but I'm African-American, and when I heard him say that, I knew I really must have been pale!

We tried to remember every minute detail, and after hearing our story he wanted to go back and see for himself if something was out there.

"No way," we both said.

Several times I have relayed this story to others, especially residents of Moloka'i. They have offered several theories about what it was we saw, the most common being that we saw a creature called the Mū, an ancient, violent, mean-spirited creature that hasn't been spotted— by anyone else, at least—in decades.

We were told to forget the incident and not repeat it to others, because the Mū have powers to do good—or evil—and might not appreciate being the object of discussion.

A long-time resident of Hawai'i, Joyce Garnes works for the Hawai'i Visitors and Convention Bureau. Traveling and meeting people are her passion and a never-ending source of delight.

If you believe, as many in Hawai'i do, that rocks have *mana* (power), you will understand what's going on in this spooky tale. A woman on Moloka'i finds herself involved in a dramatic discussion with rocks on the island's abrupt North Shore peak . . .

Oloku'i

Day after day and night after night, for about three and a half years, or around a thousand days and nights, I lived my life on the lower slopes of Oloku'i, beneath its towering height. Oloku'i faces the ocean—faces north, encircled by the Ko'olau range of Moloka'i, as if it were the *ali'i* mountain of the island, surrounded by its warriors. It forms the western wall of Wailau Valley and the eastern wall of Pelekunu Valley. The afternoons in Wailau are cut short by the shadows of Oloku'i.

Oloku'i boasts the highest sea cliffs in the world: fifteen hundred feet of volcanic blackness rising straight out of Pacific waves that travel thousands of miles before slapping up against its motionless face.

Oloku'i has a dark spirit, and while I loved my life on its lower plateau, it was sometimes an uneasy relationship. Its green slopes sparkled in the morning sun, its beauty and majesty unending, but it had its treacherous side. We heard a story of an unhappy old woman who, in Hawaiian days, lived up the hill from our camp and waited, watching the ocean for her husband who never returned. One night when I was alone in the camp, I sat strumming an ukulele and singing, and I became aware of ghostly voices from somewhere up the hill behind me, singing along. I stopped to listen, and the voices seemed to change their tone, into a mournful, plaintive howl. I put down the ukulele, lit a lamp, and read a book instead, remembering my Hawaiian friends' admonition, "No sing at night."

It was during my time in this ancient valley that I learned what the Hawaiians already knew: the land has a life and a spirit of its own, as surely as we humans do. It has power and personality and whims and moods, and we need to listen closely to the land and try to understand its needs.

I won't say that I understood what Olokuʻi was trying to tell me, but when it started throwing rocks at me, I began to pay close attention.

The first time I witnessed the heavy power of this mighty mountain, I was walking with my dog about a half-mile from our wilderness camp at the beach, on a search for mountain apples. A sudden crashing sound split the peace of the sunny morning. There was no mistaking the source of the racket: trees splitting, the thundering sound of something huge and heavy slamming to earth, and the rumble of its roll down the steep slope. It was like hearing a train roar past, but I couldn't see anything. When the crashing finally subsided, I walked a little farther on in the same direction we had been headed. There I saw a tunnel gouged out of the thick forest reaching up and down the mountainside as far as I could see in both directions. I followed the tunnel down to where the monstrous boulder had come to rest on a flat stretch of the valley floor. It was nicked and scarred from its furious flight, and I knew I had come very close to a force of nature. Or should I say it came close to me!

It was about a year later that the rock throwing grew more personal and more violent.

Early one morning, just after sunup, my husband, Bill, and I were picking up our lay-net from where we had set it out into the ocean the night before, in front of the sheer *pali* that loomed over the beach. Many days this narrow stretch of sand was completely unapproachable, assaulted by the huge north-shore surf crashing up against the *pali* wall. Even on calm days like this one, you could see where small rocks had fallen from the heights above and drilled pukas into the sand. But on this day, the fishing spot had yielded a great catch, several good-sized *kūmū* and *pāpio*, and plenty of *āholehole*. Dinner for a couple of days. We were folding the net, I was holding it out in front of me, and we were talking. The truth is, I will always remember the fact that I was bitching at Bill about something. I don't remember what it was, but I distinctly remember that I was giving him a hard time. And right in the middle of a sentence, out of nowhere and with no warning, a rock about the size of a fist slammed down onto my left hand and split open my thumb. I screamed and ran toward the *pali*, cowering against the wall, afraid that more rocks would follow, but the one that hit me that day was flying solo.

My thumb was badly smashed, and would need medical attention. During the winter, when the surf closes out the broad bay, the only way out of Wailau Valley to the civilized side of Moloka'i is an eight-hour hike over the mountain, and I was in no condition to make the trek. It took all day to signal a passing plane and finally get a rescue helicopter to take us to Moloka'i General Hospital. The danger had passed, and it was now just a matter of dealing with the injury, but the random nature of the accident had a chilling effect. What if the rock had been a few inches off course, and hit me in the head? It would have killed me, for sure. It felt like a brush with death.

Needless to say, I was in no hurry to return to that spot in front of the *pali*, that narrow little bit of sand where we had sometimes ventured at low tide in order to reach the peninsula down the coast. But one time I let that possibility cross my mind and it was during that fleeting moment that I began to think that Oloku'i truly did not want me there. I began to believe that I was being warned away, and that I needed to heed the warning. The next time old man Oloku'i threw a rock for me, he put on quite a show.

It happened one evening just after I had set the net into the ocean straight out from the beach in front of our camp. My young niece, Amanda, was with me; Bill was out of the valley getting supplies. We had not been catching much lately, so I said to Amanda, "If we don't get a good catch tonight, maybe tomorrow we'll . . . "

I turned toward the end of the beach where the mountain met the ocean, thinking that maybe I would brave the old fishing spot under the *pali* the following night.

My eyes bugged out and my jaw dropped: a boulder the size of a small car was in mid-air, flying in a long arch from the top of the *pali* toward the ocean! I could do nothing but stare and point. Amanda turned to follow my gaze. All she saw was the huge splash as the rock hit the ocean and sent up a tower of water at least fifty feet into the air.

No, I thought, I guess I won't go down there tomorrow night. Or any other time. I guess I will just keep my distance from the black ocean *pali* of Oloku'i.

Do I believe that the mountain was speaking to me? Or was it just a coincidence? After all, the eroding volcanic mountains all around the islands are constantly slipping and sliding and rolling toward the sea. Now that I live on O'ahu, I see the evidence everywhere. Now, when I see a small rock near the mouth of the Pali tunnel on O'ahu, I say a little prayer. And when I drive around Makapu'u, I hold my breath and eye the rubble beneath the cliffs there. It could happen almost anywhere.

You think what you want about whether I was receiving a warning. I won't tempt fate.

Pam Soderberg and her husband, Bill Dunn, reluctantly left Moloka'i several years ago for the big-city life of O'ahu. They now live and work in Kailua, where life is a beach.

Puʻu Kaʻana

One morning in May, before sunrise, I set out in total darkness on the island of Molokaʻi with a flashlight, bound for Puʻu Kaʻana, the sacred mountain famed in chants for *lehua* blossoms and said to be the original site where ancients learned the hula. Each year many Hawaiians from all islands come to the mountain to reenact the birth of the hula in a unique dawn ceremony impossible to attend without invitation.

It was my great good fortune to be one of very few haoles invited to this ceremony. I hardly slept at all the night before. Now Puʻu Kaʻana is the highest point in the Maunaloa Area on Molokaʻi's south side, a veritable landmark. It should have been an easy summit to find even in the dark, especially with a local guide. But somehow, we took the wrong trail, went *mauka* instead of *makai*, and got lost. By the time we found the right trail and reached Kaʻana, the hula ceremony had ended. Everyone was returning, some looking as if they'd seen a miracle. Everyone I spoke to later down at Pāpōhaku Beach Park where Ka Hula Piko Festival ensued, called the day's first event "chicken skin." And, of course, said I should have been there.

The Island of Lāna'i

The Spirits Return to Lāna'i

The Spirit of the Lodge

I spent last Halloween telling spooky stories at The Lodge at Kō'ele on Lāna'i, where it was my good luck to meet Helen Fujie, the legendary storyteller of that spirit-haunted island. I didn't recognize her at first because I expected an elderly Japanese woman. Instead, she appeared that night as a Chinese mandarin with her hair tucked under a skullcap; she had even penciled in a mascara mustache. A perfect disguise. After I read several stories to the guests I asked her, please, to tell about some of the strange things that happen when . . .

The Spirits Return to Lāna'i

An ancient Lāna'i legend told that Kaululā'au, a naughty son of one of the chiefs of Lahaina, was banished to Lāna'i across the 'Au'au Channel. He was to conquer all the evil spirits that prevented the colonization of Lāna'i. Then he could go back home to Lahaina.

He was so clever he outwitted them all and destroyed the evil spirits, one by one. Then he built a huge bonfire on the Keōmuku Beach to let his family know that all was safe now for human habitation.

But some spirits remain on Lāna'i. They are no longer evil, but they have their ancient chants and drumbeats on their night-marching trails: Mānele to Naha, over Lāna'ihale, Kaunolū, and Kaumalapau to Pālāwai and Polihua.

So campers, beware! Stay out of their way when you hear them coming—you can hear them coming, but you cannot see them. They are spirits of ancient warriors.

Some of their trails go right through the schoolgrounds toward the old Hawaiian graveyard on a plateau beyond the present cemetery area.

When the new gym (Pedro Dela Cruz Gym) was being built, the construction crew dug up some human skeletons while bulldozing the ground for its foundation. Principal Sakamoto called Revered Kaopuiki to rebury the bones and ask permission of their spirits to let the gym be built.

Up to that time, the mechanics could not figure out how and why all the equipment broke down—caterpillars and fingerlifts turned over, and the crane collapsed.

After Reverend Kaopuiki's Hawaiian prayers, everything worked well up to his lei-cutting opening ceremony blessings. Children have reported some harmless ghostly sightings in the gym's bathrooms during the night games.

At the Mānele Black Sand Beach, when the army engineers tried to dredge the bay to build a breakwater of huge boulders and tried to pound piles for the piers or boat slips, their machinery all broke down.

Nothing worked until Reverend Kaopuiki suggested that the fishermen and boatmen who needed this storm haven hold a luau. Their first offering of *kālua* pig was made near the *pipi* (cattle) chute and the *pa'akai* (salt) flat, just above the bay where an ancient *heiau* used to be.

The very next day, after the luau, everything worked well. The spirits of the area tried to conserve the bay as is, to protect their *kuleana* (property). It took a Hawaiian priest to plead to them asking permission to improve the area.

The former Kaumalapau Harbor used to be heavily damaged—many boats and the pier itself were hit by the huge, raging waves that came from the south. They came over the breakwater like Niagara Falls and lifted the concrete harbor walls, moving everything about and smashing boats at the bottom of the cliffs of Kaumalapau. With Reverend Kaopuiki's blessing, the Mānele Bay Boat Harbor became a safe haven, especially during *kona* storms.

Most of the spirits of Lāna'i now exist as night marchers, who are not evil but curious and mischievous. They go through people's homes, opening windows and doors, cabinets and drawers, banging and slamming but never disturbing or damaging anything as the poltergeists are known to do around the world, levitating heavy furniture or throwing things around.

These Hawaiian night marchers chant and drum their way through Lāna'i City, too. Several people have heard them coming, but no one has ever seen them. One can hear the rustling of the leaves under their marching feet. The cats and dogs "feel" them coming, so their fur coats stiffen at the scruff of their neck—they snarl at the "unseen."

A retired school teacher and administrator, Helen Fujie writes regularly for the *Lanai Times* and occasionally for the *Honolulu Advertiser*. Born and raised in Kahului, Maui, she is a graduate of the University of Hawai'i College of Education. She taught on Lāna'i for forty years and worked as a substitute teacher and volunteer until 1996. She and husband Roy K. Fujie have three sons and two granddaughters. Her stories "Roy and Pele," "Katsup," and "Cowboy Kauwenaole" appeared in *Hawai'i's Best Spooky Tales*.

A sophisticated world traveler from San Francisco, not one to be shaken by ghost stories, Ms. Harrison heard about strange things that happen in the Lodge at Kōʻele on the spirit-haunted island of Lānaʻi, but she dismissed all stories as poppycock designed to scare a woman alone. That night, in her room, she felt someone, something, in her bed and discovered . . .

The Spirit of the Lodge

Several years ago, my work carried me frequently to Lāna'i, one of the most remote islands in the world. There is no instrument landing system on Lāna'i, so if the pilot cannot see the airport runway, the plane can't land. I have been on a plane from Honolulu that tried to make the dip to get below the clouds and failed, turning back to O'ahu.

When the tiny plane does land—and you must sit on the port side for the best view incoming and starboard outgoing—it comes in parallel to the length of the island, past steep cliffs that rush straight down to the gently pounding ocean, then skims the brilliantly hued red dirt and green fields and glides onto the short runway. Lāna'i is the only place I've been where the airline worker welcomes me back with a hug each time he sees me walk from the tarmac into the small airport.

This 141-square-mile island, once planted with twenty thousand acres of pineapple, bears not a single traffic light nor fast-food franchise. The first ATM machine was recently installed in the ambitiously named Lāna'i City, whose town square is surrounded by shops supplied weekly by a barge that arrives from Honolulu. Everyone knows that the Häagen-Dazs shipment arrives on Thursday; it has a shelf life of about two hours before it's sold out.

Lāna'i City is home to two thousand residents, most of whom are of Filipino descent. The older ones came to the island to "pick pine" and work in the fields when pineapple was king. They live in brightly painted wooden plantation-style houses with tin roofs and riotous vegetation in their front yards. There is no need to lock doors. They have abundant family and fertile gardens, they talk story and lead simple lives.

Once known as the Pineapple Island, Lāna'i now tends two luxury resorts, The Lodge at Kō'ele and Mānele Bay Hotel, both lauded as among the best in the world. I was headed to the former, an upcountry lodge exuding quiet elegance, serving gourmet food, and displaying more orchids than Kew Gardens. I would be leaving Hawai'i soon, and I had come to sleep with the ghosts.

It had been reported by several female guests that ghosts occupied a particular room at the Lodge. These women claim to have felt the ghost's presence, and one even saw its face. The general manager had also received reports from housekeeping—one maid said she had been bitten.

Skeptical, I demanded the very same room for my one night on the island. It was available, and I was given the key. "You can't think about them, or they won't come," said Kurt Matsumoto, general manager. "And they come only at night."

No sweat. I enjoyed dinner—seared wild venison from the island and some heady red wine, then returned to my room. Once in bed, I turned out the lights. A raging silence, then some small noises. I poked my head out from the covers and saw, somewhat to my relief, nothing. I hid farther down under the Belgian cotton sheets and realized I was scared. Even worse, I was wide awake.

I must have drifted off to sleep, because I was jarred awake by the buzzing of the alarm clock. I had not set the alarm, so assumed it must have been set by the previous guest. But it was midnight. The first plane off the island leaves at 6 A.M., and the airport is a mere ten minutes away. Why would anyone set the alarm for midnight? Goose bumps—what locals call chicken skin—began to appear.

I got out of bed, sheepishly looking around corners and behind doors on my way to the bathroom. I was cold as ice. This is upcountry Hawai'i, and a chill in the air is normal, but this was definitely polar. I crept back into bed, turned off the lights, and shut my eyes tight. As for what happened next, all I know is what I remembered when I woke the next morning.

What I remember is this: There was something in bed with me, on either side of my body, and whatever it was, it was pushing me from both sides, as if to move me out of the bed. Each time it pushed, I felt something, an energy, pass through my body. I recall being half-awakened each time it happened, and each time my unconscious thought was, "It's only the ghosts; they're passing through."

Legend has it that, as a punishment for misbehaving, the son of the king of Maui was banished to the island of Lāna'i, a land filled with terrible spirits. But he triumphed over the spirits, built a bonfire as a sign of his success, and was welcomed back home. I, too, had triumphed over the spirits and would be welcomed home, although I didn't realize it at the time.

I left Hawai'i for San Francisco a few days later. Over the next month, a string of unexpected events occurred. Doors once shut tight began to slowly crack open. I reconnected with my parents after a seven-year estrangement. I accepted a book contract. I was finally becoming myself.

It's as if the ghosts were crying, "Don't go back to sleep."

Babs Harrison, a former writer for *The Dallas Morning News*, is the author of *The Lion in the Moon: Two Against the Sahara, Exploring New Mexico Wine Country,* and, forthcoming in 1999, *Kitschy Cocktails: Luscious Libations for the Swinger Set* and *Kitschy Canapés: Finger Foods for the Swinger Set*. A Texas native, she lived on Oʻahu for three years and now commutes from San Francisco.

The Island of Hawai'i

Under a full moon, a young man freshly arrived in Hawai'i soaks up the beauty, power, and spirituality of the Big Island's Kohala Coast on the beach one night with new friends. Later that night, alone in his room, he is disturbed by a dream that the world is ending and awakes to find night marchers passing through his room. Years later, he mentions his dream to a Hawaiian *kupuna* and discovers an eerie coincidence in this bone-chilling tale that makes you wonder . . .

Is the End Near?

My love affair with the Big Island started on a moon-lit night at the far end of a wide crescent of beach in front of the Mauna Kea Beach Hotel. I lounged half in, half out of the warm, gently lapping waters with two new friends, Zeke and Donna. The palm fronds above our heads danced and rustled in the trade winds, and the moon was bright between the Big Island and Maui.

We talked of life, how its turns are fast and unexpected, and how it's all too easy to forget to do exactly what we were then doing: partaking of the pleasures of earth's golden corners. We talked awhile and then we stopped and merely sat, listening to the waves softly splash on the sand and the palms whisper in the sweet-smelling air.

To call Hawai'i beautiful is accurate, but wholly inadequate, particularly in regard to the Big Island, where extreme beauty, spirituality, and natural power combine with Hawaiian history and culture. I had a taste of them all that night in 1987.

We lingered for quite some time, talking some, but mainly listening to the big silence that one can hear on Hawai'i.

Later that night I had a dream I recall to this day as vividly as if I had it but last night. In the dream I walked down to a grassy ledge above the Pacific to watch a strange dusk. Everyone I had ever known in my life was there, friends from long ago, family living and gone. They were gathered in small groups around all the prophets and sages that have ever walked the earth—Jesus, Mohammed, Gandhi, and others. I walked in and out of these groups and listened to what they were discussing. Each group had the same topic: the end of the world.

There was no fear in these discussions, only curiosity and the desire for knowledge. Charcoal clouds swirled in the bloody sky. I walked to the cliff and looked out: the Pacific was red and boiling.

The images were not disturbing to me, but significant—why, I did not know. They caused me to wake up, and when I did, there were spirits in my room. At the foot of the bed several spirits were marching by in procession. The one in the lead carried a torch. They were silent. A voice from somewhere inside told me not to fear them, and I believed it. The procession passed onto the lanai and vanished.

Eleven years later I told this experience to Danny Akaka, whose Mauna Lani business card reads Hawaiian Historian, but who is more than that. Danny is one of a handful of Hawaiians who caretake the traditions and culture of these islands as their life's work, and a spiritual man whom you immediately trust.

His response changed me as much as the dream and vision had changed me more than a decade earlier. "I have had similar dreams," he said, "ever since Kīlauea began its current eruption.

"Believe me, I am not an alarmist," he told me. "And I'm not trying to scare anyone. But I believe your dream is a prophecy. I believe the volcano will change this island dramatically. And it will change many people's lives. That is why the ocean is red and boiling.

"I don't know when this will happen," he said. "But I

believe these things are true."

Even though I do not live there, I call the Big Island my spiritual home. Things happen there as they happen few other places in the world. The ancient Yaqui Indians believed that the earth is criss-crossed with lines of power, and where these lines intersect the power is strongest. Perhaps that is what we feel on the Big Island of Hawai'i—lines of power intersecting.

The Hawaiian people, too, know the power of the Big Island, and of the fire goddess Pele. Kīlauea's decade-long (and ongoing) eruption is evidence of that. Whether Danny Akaka's premonition of change is right or not remains to be seen. But one thing is sure: anything can happen on the Big Island of Hawai'i.

Hawai'i resident George Fuller is currently editor and publisher of ASIA-PACIFIC GOLF, a golf travel and lifestyle magazine focusing on the courses of Asia and the Pacific Rim. The author of five books, he has also written and edited countless books and articles for book publishers, newspapers, and magazines in Hawai'i and the Pacific.

According to traditional Hawaiian belief, any element of a person's body is of paramount importance because it contains the person's *mana*, or mystic power. Even something as seemingly insignificant as a nail clipping can be used to cause harm to someone—and even to pray him to death. Imagine, then, the power contained in a person's mortal remains. This is why so many burials are hidden and why the location of the bones of Kamehameha the Great remains known only to the moon and the stars to this very day. All these thoughts began to occur to a young woman on the Big Island one summer day after she accepted a rare invitation to visit a Hawaiian burial cave and step back to . . .

A Moment in Time

 It was just past 2:30 on a scorching July afternoon. I'd gobbled the last handful of my daily allotment of M&Ms and was sipping the bottom half of my third cup of coffee while waiting for the coffee-and-sugar rush to kick in. Writing up notes from a press conference I'd attended that morning was the most exciting task ahead of me that day. And then a call came into the Neighbor Island news-room that still gives me chills to think about fifteen years later.

The voice on the other end of the line said he'd been following my reporting for the community newspaper and thought I was a fair, ethical person who understood and respected Hawaiian history, culture, and beliefs. He said he wanted to show me a place that had been important to his family for centuries. He wanted to take me to the underground burial place of his ancestors, and he wanted me to bring a photographer.

The next half hour was a blur of hurried conversations with the editor and the photographer. We piled into a truck and stopped by my apartment so I could change into shorts and hiking shoes. Then we met the caller, who explained why he wanted strangers to visit the burial site.

The landowner was planning a shopping center and gas station on the acreage. The area was rocky lava; any construction would involve smoothing the blocky lava

flow and extensive excavating to accommodate the subterranean fuel tanks for the gas station.

After we parked along the highway and walked around
and through countless patches of scrub brush and lava
clinker, our escort hesitantly asked us to wear bandannas
over our eyes briefly so we wouldn't see the path leading
to the entrance to the lava tube that was the burial
chamber.

The absence of sight enhanced my other senses—the
coarse lava clinker crunched and crackled loudly under-
foot, the sun seared through my white cotton shirt, and
the soft, well-washed bandanna covering my eyes was
oddly comforting. My steps slowed, and then it was time
to take off the bandanna and descend into the lava tube.

The air was cool and slightly musty—it took little
imagination to sense that the air of centuries surrounded
us—and soon I was swathed in a blanket of black. I was
stepping so carefully that I was upon the remains in what
seemed an instant. Even after fifteen years, I see them
clearly still. The details are etched in my memory,
although I've hesitated to discuss them, restrained by a
complicated blend of respect, awe, and unvarnished superstition.

The woman was prepared for her voyage and laid to
rest in a canoe-like vessel that had been placed on a shelf
within the lava tube. I believe the person to whom these
mortal remains belonged was loved in life and honored in
death. Although I have thought of her often in the last
decade and a half, I have never felt the need to speculate
about who exactly she was and in what era she lived. It has
been enough for me to know that she had walked the
same lands hundreds of years ago, that she wore her hair
almost waist length, and that she was no taller than I.

After a short time our guide aimed the beam of the

flashlight toward the exit, and we ascended to daylight and the everyday world. The photographer and I drove back to the office in silence, and when my hands stopped shaking, I began typing notes on my computer. After a telephone interview with the landowner's representative, I wrote a front-page article describing my experience and stating the positions of our guide and his family—and of the developer.

Today, the shopping center and gas station do land-office business. I do not know whether the burial was disturbed in the process, or whether, as the developer stated, the cave was beyond the area encompassed by the development. I do know that whenever the subject of disturbing human remains arises, I'm struck into silence that comes from wondering what happened to the woman from another century.

Award-winning writer and editor Camie Foster is a lifelong Hawai'i resident. Among her honors are a Pacific Asia Travel Association Gold Award for the top travel story in a hotel magazine, several awards from the Hawai'i Publishers Association, and an award from the Hawai'i Visitors & Convention Bureau for a long-running column about everyday life in the Islands. She has edited the *Hawai'i Hotel Network* since 1986 and is currently Hawai'i bureau chief for *Travel Agent* Magazine.

Everyone needs directions
when traveling interisland, as
three Honolulu women
discover when they meet an
old Hawaiian man
in Kailua-Kona
Airport on . . .

A Moonless Night in Kona

It happened during Thanksgiving weekend, 1967, in Kona. I was working for a travel organization in Waikīkī. My job entailed offering recommendations to visitors on places to see, things to do, and hotels to stay in.

About three times a year, my two co-workers, Juanita and Aulani, and I would plan a trip to one of the neighbor islands over a long weekend to stay familiar with new hotels, tours, etc.

We had spent about two weeks planning our upcoming trip to the Big Island. Because of its size, we drew a map of the Big Island and marked all the places we would be stopping at around the island, figuring this would make it much easier for us once we were on the road.

Aulani and Juanita decided to make this a "fun trip" and asked their husbands to join us. As usual, airline reservations were tight: Juanita and I were able to get on a 5:00 P.M. flight to Kona, but we had to wait until approximately 9:00 P.M. for Aulani and the two husbands, who were arriving on a private plane.

Juanita and I sat in the old Kona airport talking and passing the time watching people come and go. I pulled our map out of my bag a couple of times to review some of the stops we'd be making. As darkness fell, the crowds thinned out. By 8:00 the final commercial flight had come and gone and workers were locking up for the night. An

Aloha Airlines employee came up to see if we needed assistance; when we told him we were waiting for a private plane, he smiled and told us we were in the perfect spot since the private planes landed right outside.

After he left, I was spooked, because no one else was in the terminal! I decided to sit across from Juanita so she could watch my back and vice versa. It was eerie. The parking lot was pitch black, and the lights on the runway were dull and looked as if they were dancing. And the quiet—it was oh, so quiet. I kept looking at Juanita and she kept looking at me, both of us trying to put up a brave front!

I turned to the right and looked out onto the runway. It was a moonless night, the ocean was calm, and I could see the silhouette of a *kiawe* tree against the dark sky. I was mesmerized by this scene. Then a movement down by the *kiawe* tree caught my eye. I blinked to make sure I wasn't seeing things. Yup, there was movement down there. I could see figures walking along the shoreline at the edge of the runway.

Wait a minute! I could see men wearing *mahiole* and feather capes. They looked like warriors! There was no sound. It hit me like a lightning bolt! These were night marchers, a long procession of them. The hair on the back of my neck stood up. I was as white as a sheet! Juanita was trying to talk to me, and I kept telling her to be quiet, not to make a sound.

All the stories I had heard from my *tūtū* and my dad came to mind. I kept pointing to the procession and telling Juanita about the movement, but she kept telling me there was nothing there. I don't know how she could have missed them.

I was quite shaken after this experience. Juanita and I were both scared. I sat completely still in my chair and would not look out at the runway. I was looking straight ahead and could see someone approaching, walking toward me. He was an older Hawaiian gentleman, slim, with white hair and dark skin, wearing a long-sleeved white shirt, a *lauhala* hat, and long pants. He was walking, but he wasn't making a sound. How can that be, I thought.

I was trying to tell Juanita that he was coming from behind her, but no sound would come out of my mouth. This gentleman walked right up to me and said, "Aloha." He had a dazzling smile.

I answered by saying, "Aloha, how are you?"

He said, "I came to get the map that you have in your purse." I was dumbfounded!

Juanita, in the meantime, asked him where he came from. He replied, "I come from Hilo and I have to get the map."

With that, I got the map out of my purse and handed it to him. He took it from my hand and thanked me. Juanita then asked him where he was going and he said, "I'm going back to Hilo." Then, he turned and began to walk away from me. He walked about ten feet and then disappeared into thin air!

This completely unraveled us! We didn't know where to turn or what to do because we were the only people at the airport. Soon we heard a plane approaching. When it landed, we ran to greet our friends.

Upon overhearing our story, an elderly Hawaiian woman walked up to me and told me not to fret. "Those night marchers were your *'ohana*, welcoming you to the place of your family's beginnings. Don't fear them, embrace them, for they will watch over you during your stay here.

"As for the gentleman who took your map, he was

your 'aumakua, who took the form of a human. Danger was awaiting you at one of the sites marked on your map, and he was protecting you."

Having said that, she got into a car and drove off.

Madelyn Horner Fern was born and raised on Oʻahu. A graduate of the Kamehameha Schools, she is the mother of three grown children and works as Human Resources Manager at the Sheraton Maui Hotel.

The King's Trail

A groove in the dirt three feet deep runs along the Big Island's Kohala Coast for miles. The Ala Loa, or King's Trail, looks as if somebody ran a unicycle along the shore, until you realize this path was cut by thousands of bare feet long ago.

This trail of old Hawai'i takes in lava caves, C-shaped windbreaks, freshwater springs, pocket coves, fishponds, traps, and shrines. One of the finest and largest concentrations of stone symbols of the Pacific, more than three thousand petroglyphs line the route like old graffiti. A fifteen-acre slate bed of smooth *pāhoehoe* lava at Ka'upulehu includes rare images of twins, a surfing fisherman, and mysterious sails that inspired the logo of nearby Kona Village, my favorite Big Island haunt.

Go, walk in the footsteps of ancients, see Hawai'i the way it was before fantasy resorts and eighteen-hole championship golf courses; take a walk on The King's Trail.

While her colleagues press on into the uninhabited valleys of the Big Island's Kohala Coast, a weary backpacker remains behind in Honokāne Valley enjoying the solitude— until she hears the faint strumming of a guitar and looks around to discover no one there, only . . .

The Spirit of Honokāne

I was born and raised in North Kohala on the Big Island of Hawai'i, and as a child spent many hours playing on the black sand beach of Pololū Valley. This is a remote, wet valley (previously used to grow taro and rice) on the windward side of North Kohala, where the road ends at a scenic overlook. No one has lived in this valley and the other valleys to the east for years.

During the summer of 1973, I was an archaeology student at the University of Hawai'i at Mānoa, doing research in Pololū Valley on a National Science Foundation stipend. The other researchers and I also backpacked into Honokāne Nui, the next valley over, and Honokāne Iki, the smaller valley east of Honokāne Nui. So I was familiar with these uninhabited valleys and their trails. I lived in Pololū for three months that summer and continued to hike into the valley thereafter.

Several years later I decided to hike with three other friends into the valley. We hiked into Pololū, then over into Honokāne Nui. I do not recollect meeting anyone on the trail into the second valley. The others wanted to see Honokāne Iki, but since I was tired, I chose to stay by myself on the pebbly beach of Honokāne Nui.

I was sunning myself on the deserted beach when

suddenly I heard loud guitar strumming. I sat up and looked around and shouted, "Who's there?" There was no answer. I was startled because I did not see anyone on the beach near me, but the guitar strumming continued.

I looked up into the sky. There was no plane or helicopter or anything near me. Then the strumming stopped. I did not see anyone else on that beach.

When my three friends returned about half an hour later, I did not tell them of the incident, as I was afraid they would scoff at me. Incidentally, none of us had a guitar with us.

We then hiked up the ridge between Honokāne Nui and Pololū and then way into the back of Pololū to a secret swimming hole I knew of. While we were eating lunch and swimming at this pool, which is way off the main trail, one of my *haole* friends turned to me and said, "I hear a guitar strumming."

I stared at him and felt chicken skin go down my back. I couldn't hear the guitar he was talking about and neither could the other two people. Then I told them about what had occurred on the beach of Honokāne Nui, now miles away.

Frightened by this mysterious guitar strumming, we quickly packed up our knapsacks and hiked out of Pololū. We didn't hear any guitar strumming after that, and did not see anyone on the trail out of Pololū Valley, but we felt that a spirit had been following us on the trails.

Carolyn Sugiyama Classen graduated from Kohala High School, the University of Hawai'i-Mānoa, and Boston College Law School. She currently lives in Tucson, Arizona, and Hilo, Hawai'i. She is a tribal staff attorney for the Pascua Yaqui Tribe of Arizona.

When two of Hawai'i's best storytellers pay a visit to Hawai'i Volcanoes National Park, they agree, out of respect for Madame Pele, not to tell traditional Pele stories. It seemed like the right thing to do. When they ignore Madame Pele completely and tell stories of others, strange things begin to happen in this spooky tale . . .

At the Volcano's Edge

Christmas, 1988. My friend and fellow Native Hawaiian storyteller, Woody Fern, and I were invited by the Volcano Art Center to do two storytelling performances at the Hawai'i Volcanoes National Park.

We took an early flight to Hilo, checked in at Uncle Billy's Hilo Bay Hotel, and proceeded in our brand new subcompact rental car to the park, some twenty-five miles out of Hilo town. Our road led through what was once the great Pana'ewa Forest. Out of respect for the "Lady," Woody and I had both agreed that we would not tell traditional legends about Pele; rather, we would tell stories of Hawai'i's history and stories of Pele's sister, Hi'iaka, who had battled the *mo'o* Pana'ewa somewhere in these forested regions.

Our first performance was to take place in the morning at an overlook near the crater's rim. Seated with the rim at our backs, we told stories of Princess Ruth, Hi'iaka and Pana'ewa, Big Island sharks, Robert Louis Stevenson in Hawai'i, and many others to fifteen or twenty park visitors. The sky was clear, and everything seemed peaceful. We returned to Hilo to rest, shower, and have dinner.

That evening Woody and I were to return to do a Christmas program at the Kīlauea Military Camp Theatre for guests of an Elderhostel tour. The program would begin at 7:30 that evening. At 6:30 it was already quite dark as we drove back toward the volcano. As we traveled along the highway through a stretch of the old Pana'ewa Forest, suddenly the car engine began to sputter and the car stalled several times before surging to life again. Perhaps it was a portent, but the rest of the ride was uneventful, though our minds were filled with unspoken thoughts.

That evening we told Christmas stories and pidgin English stories to a delighted group of a hundred. After the program was over, we were making our way back to the car in the parking lot when I noticed that I was missing the earring from my left ear. I had borrowed that earring from my daughter especially for this performance. It was silver and had been purchased from an art museum on the mainland as a gift for her. I was sure I had had the earring on at the beginning of the performance.

Our host and Woody accompanied an embarrassed me back to the theater, where we searched the stage and everywhere else I had been that evening. Having no luck, we returned to the car, where I ran my hands over every inch of the car's seats, between the seats, along the floors, and even in the paneling of the doors. The earring was NOT there!

Woody was quite concerned and offered to take out his mini mag-flashlight and help me search. The flashlight was in a briefcase that looked like a zippered pouch about ten inches by fifteen inches. Woody unzipped the case and felt inside for the flashlight. He couldn't find it. He turned his briefcase upside down and emptied the contents on the car seat. There were his pens, papers, and pencils, but no flashlight!

We returned to the hotel that evening, and I dreaded telling my daughter about her lost earring. Woody had emptied his briefcase once more back in his hotel room and searched his luggage for the flashlight—but it had simply disappeared! As I returned to my room, I said a little prayer that we would find these lost items and asked forgiveness if we had offended.

The next morning we packed and met in the lobby to catch the flight back to Honolulu. We carried our luggage out to the car in the parking lot. While Woody stowed the luggage in the trunk, I went to unlock the doors. There, right in the middle of the passenger-side seat, as if laid out for me to find, was the silver earring, glinting in the light of the early morning sun. It hadn't been there the night before.

I knew how thoroughly I had searched. I had run my hands over every inch of that seat searching for that earring. Now here it was twenty-five miles away from the place where I had lost it! How had it come to be placed in a locked car, twenty-five miles away, on the following morning? It was mystifying. I said a quiet "Mahalo" and we drove to the airport.

I had felt so bad about Woody losing his mag-flashlight, I told my husband when I got home that we would have to buy Woody another one. A few days later, however, Woody called. He had opened his briefcase at home and out fell his flashlight. Had it been there all that time—or had it just been returned?

Perhaps we should have given the "Lady" her due and told HER stories at the crater's rim—HER home. We do not know. Was it a warning or was it only a playful prank to remind these two modern storytellers that the old stories and the ancient places still have *mana*?

Of Native Hawaiian and Asian ancestry, Nyla Fujii-Babb has been a professional storyteller, actress, and librarian in Hawai'i for twenty years.

The morning was bright, the trade winds soft but insistent. Her husband, tired from the stress of work and from the long flight, snoozed in their room. She went for a sunrise walk on the beach. She thought she heard clear, high voices, singing. Was it . . .

A Kohala Kyrie

It was early in December, and we—my husband Ted and I—were staying at the Mauna Kea Beach Hotel on the Big Island. For as long as I have been coming to Hawai'i—which is going on thirty years—I have loved to walk the beach at sunrise. This particular December morning was calm and bright, the sky empty of clouds, the sun still below the long, slow rise of the mountain called Mauna Kea, for which the resort is named. The long curve of beach was empty, except for a lone jogger at the far end. I moved out to the froth line in the easy-walking wet sand.

It was the Hawai'i I love best, the crest of the waves turning a slow rose pink, the changing colors of the ocean and the sky, the vast blueness of it all. Above me, close by, a seabird wheeled and slid on the wind. I breathed deeply of it all and felt it spread through me, luminous: Hawai'i. It was at that moment that I heard the music, very soft, very solemn. I stopped short, turned my head this way, then turned it back; the music faded in and faded out.

Christmas music, I thought. It sounded like a boy's choir singing liturgical music, a kyrie eleison. Sweet little high-pitched voices in exquisite harmony. I walked down the beach, letting the music rise and fall. It seemed to be coming from a grove of trees at the far end of the beach.

Practice, I thought, that's it—a choir is practicing for a Christmas program. I made my way over, slowed by the effort of walking in deeper dry sand, but when I reached the trees they were empty. No one was there, no one at all.

What could you be thinking, I asked myself. Choir practice at six in the morning? And yet as I stood there all alone, my head tilted just so, the exquisite music echoed through me.

The lone jogger was approaching now, a young woman with a sleek, hard body. I considered asking her to stop and listen with me, but I didn't. I suppose because of a nagging worry that she wouldn't hear anything at all.

For perhaps half an hour I stayed on the beach, enjoying the high, sweet voices soaring in ecclesiastical song. Then I made my way back to our room, to wake Ted and tell him about it.

He listened carefully, as always, and, being given to logical explanations, finally came up with, "Well, sound waves are peculiar, especially over water."

But I could see that he wasn't convinced, and neither was I. We've been coming to Hawai'i long enough to know you shouldn't expect answers to everything. Sometimes you have, simply, to accept some things as gifts, and that is what I decided to do. On that morning, I happily received the ethereal music as a kind of gift from Hawai'i, and maybe even as a sign that I was a welcome visitor to these magic isles.

Shirley Streshinsky is the author of *Gift of the Golden Mountain*, a complex romantic novel set in Hawai'i, and *I Alone Survived*, which became a television movie. She lives in Northern California with her photojournalist husband, Ted, and frequently writes about Hawai'i for newspapers and magazines.

Driving around the Big Island of Hawai'i from Paradise Park to Mauna Kea Beach Hotel may seem idyllic if you're on vacation. When it's your daily commute to work, it becomes a monotonous four-hour drive five days a week. One afternoon, near the ghost sugar town of Honoka'a, a young Hawaiian woman heading home experiences something she still can't explain . . .

The Lost Family of Honoka'a

In 1985 I lived on the Big Island of Hawai'i about twenty minutes outside of Hilo in an area called Paradise Park. I had launched my hotel career and was fortunate to have the opportunity to work at the beautiful and majestic Mauna Kea Beach Hotel in Kawaihae.

Unfortunately, the travel distance from my home in Paradise Park was approximately two hours one way, traversing the Hāmākua Coast through Honoka'a, Kamuela, and every little community along the way.

After a while the drive, although scenic, grew monotonous—until one late afternoon as I was traveling back home.

I'm not quite sure where I was exactly, but I do remember that it was close to Honoka'a. At this particular spot, the highway splits, the two lanes divided by a grassy median strip.

As I drove past I noticed four people, actually a family— a man, a woman, a little boy, and a little girl. This was not unusual. I often spotted hitchhikers on my drives to and from work. But these people didn't look like hitchhikers. What was unusual was the way they were dressed. All four wore mostly black clothing. The man and the boy wore starched white shirts; the woman and girl wore dark dresses and black bonnets.

I automatically began to slow down, thinking that it could possibly be an Amish family, but then realized how could that be? As I came closer, I could see that their clothing looked freshly ironed, as though they were on their way to church or a special gathering.

When I was almost alongside them, my gaze fell on the man. To my amazement, as I stared at his face what appeared to me was an outline of a face in falling ashes. The gray ash that fell from his shadowy face appeared to be falling toward the ground.

As I passed him, I felt as though for an instant I had been suspended in time.

My first thought as I began to speed up was not to look in the rearview mirror, thinking that if I looked back they surely would be gone. Instead, I did look back and to my amazement they stood there, perfectly still, patiently waiting.

Stephanie Kaluahine Reid and her family make their home in Hanalei on the island of Kauaʻi. Now in the hotel industry for thirteen years, she is director of public relations for Princeville Resort.

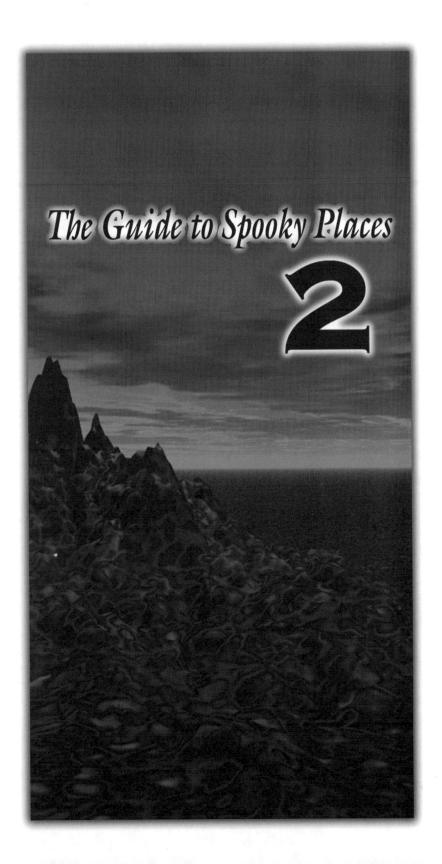

The Guide to Spooky Places

2

Once, centuries ago, Hawai'i was a land of superstition, *kapu* (taboos), animist spirits, and gloriously occult vengeance. When Captain James Cook made the mistake in 1779 of landing on the Big Island from a counterclockwise direction—after previously having sailed, more auspiciously, clockwise—he became embroiled in a dispute with angry, frightened locals and wound up hacked to death. The murder site remained haunted for years.

The Hawaiian Islands obviously are a very different place today. There are more Baptists than animists. Christian churches stand on old rocks of sacrificial altars. And you can sail into Kealakekua Bay, where Cook met his end, from any direction without undesirable consequences.

Yet Hawai'i remains rich with mysterious sites, inexplicable events, and rituals to which outsiders are not invited. Ancient ways of Hawai'i's pagan culture loom just below the surface of modern island life. *Kāhuna* (priests) still talk to rocks; the rocks, they say, talk back. Sharks embody the spirits of long-dead but still fractious relatives. And ancestral ghosts are prayed to, in hopes they'll halt construction projects, especially golf courses.

The truly adventurous traveler, or even local resident, will want to experience at least a little of this to know "chicken skin" (the local expression for "goose bumps").

That's why I created The Guide to Spooky Places for the original collection of *Hawai'i's Best Spooky Tales*, citing twenty-five places, complete with directions, maps, and a brief site description.

Some folks, I suspected, want to experience firsthand the chilling impact of authentic historic and cultural sites of Hawai'i: murder scenes, graveyards, and haunted houses, ancient *heiau* (temples), paths of night marchers, or hidden lava caves full of old bones and feather cloaks—although I refuse to reveal whereabouts of burial caves out of respect.

When *Hawai'i's Best Spooky Tales*, with The Guide to Spooky Places, became a best-seller, I knew thousands of folks were eager to discover the real and surreal Hawai'i.

By popular demand, I now present twenty-one more places guaranteed to give you chicken skin. Places like the 1779 murder scene of Captain Cook on Kealakekua Bay. The Moana Hotel room where Jane Stanford died a terrible death by poisoning. Or the haunted missionary house of Levi Chamberlain, who died in his bed.

And then there are the *wahi pana*, or sacred places of Hawai'i. The mile-high summit of Maui's Pu'u Kukui, which the people of old believed was the intersection between heaven and earth. Moloka'i's Pu'u Ka'ana, birthplace of the hula, which throbs with *mana*. The amazing Luahiwa petroglyphs of Lāna'i, which seem to come alive. And who knows what lurks around the edges of Lanikūhonua after dark?

You may never have heard of some of these places, but they have always been there, as sure as Diamond Head. Such places seldom appear in Hawai'i guidebooks (some can be discovered only if you're in the right state of mind), yet these are the places of old Hawai'i.

So, come, take the supernatural tour where paradise is full of peril, where spirits roam and enemies become fishhooks, and where that person standing behind you at the luau may not be a person after all.

O'AHU

'Iolani Palace (see page 7)

Pele's Chair (see page 27)

Pearl Harbor (see page 35)

O'ahu Cemetery

I am standing in O'ahu Cemetery, a 35-acre burial ground of old Honolulu's who's who. More a garden than a Golgotha, this 250-year-old cemetery built on a former Nu'uanu taro patch is the final resting place of sugar barons and sea captains, musicians and missionaries. It's full of true, spooky tales of the past.

Look, there are the graves of sugar baron James Campbell and railroad builder Benjamin Franklin Dillingham. Here, under shade trees beside old carriage trails are Damons, Judds, and Thurstons, the missionaries who stayed on in the islands to do good and did so well; and patriarchs of Hawai'i's first foreign families—Blaisdell, Dudoit, Farrington, Magoon, Stangenwald, and Wilder, whose names now appear on Honolulu buildings and street signs. Sleep well, dear departed pioneers.

A few grave markers give sketchy details of death: a British sea captain spilled from his horse; a nine-year-old girl drowned off Kaua'i, a Boston missionary, the victim of consumption; an army private killed in Kalalau looking for a leper. It is all there, carved in stone, old obituaries and grim reminders of mortality. Go at sunset when the last rays of the day cast eerie shadows in this old colonial boneyard.

Levi Chamberlain's Mission House

For years, I drove past the two-story white Chamberlain House on Kapi'olani Boulevard at Mission Houses Museum never suspecting that the late Levi Chamberlain, who died in the house in 1849, is still very much present. Chamberlain opens and shuts windows on the second floor, turns lights on and off, rearranges his desk, and opens the Bible to his favorite passages, according to two eyewitnesses.

A single man who arrived in Hawai'i in 1823 to serve as business agent for the New England missionaries, Chamberlain grew so lonely and dour, according to missionary accounts of the day, that four single white women—Hawai'i's first mail-order brides—were sent on a sailing ship 'round the Horn from Boston for his approval. He chose one and the rejected three returned 'round the Horn.

One dark and stormy night just before Halloween a few years ago, I told spooky tales in The Chamberlain House and nothing extraordinary happened, but the air did feel close, and I felt faint. It was probably just the humidity, but I was glad to get out of there at the end of the evening.

Kapaemahu Stones (Wizard Stones)

Near Olympic champion Duke Kahanamoku's statue stand four huge stones in the sand, often draped with wet beach towels drying in the hot, tropic sun. Those irreverent louts who use the stones for a towel rack should know that the "wizard stones" (also known as Kapaemahu Stones) are relics of old Waikīkī. The stones apparently were brought here in the fourteenth century by Tahitian priests—Kapaemahu, Kahaloa, Kapuni, and

Kinohi, who lived in Hawai'i before the reign of O'ahu's ancient ruler Kakuhihewa. The stones were believed to have healing powers for those who touched them. Those who trust in the *mana* (power) of the Wizard Stones place bright flower leis on them out of respect. You should too.

Kūkaniloko

Two rows of eighteen lava rocks once flanked a central birthing stone where women of old Hawai'i gave birth to potential *ali'i* on the Leilehua plateau. The rocks, according to belief, held the power to ease the pain of childbirth.

The rocks, many with bowl-like shapes, and some bearing petroglyphs of human forms and circles, now lie strewn in a coconut grove in a Dole pineapple field at this, the most sacred site in central O'ahu.

Birth rituals involved forty-eight chiefs who pounded drums to announce the arrival of newborns likely to become chiefs. Children born here were taken to Holonopahu Heiau, now destroyed in the pineapple field, where chiefs ceremoniously cut the umbilical cord.

Some think Kūkaniloko also may have served as an ancient astronomy site, sort of a Hawaiian Stonehenge, a place to chart a young *ali'i*'s destiny, perhaps.

Lanikūhonua

A special place for Hawaiians, Lanikūhonua (its Hawaiian name means "where the heavens meet the earth"), is a coastal retreat on the Wai'anae Coast that fairly throbs with *mana*. Ask anyone who's been there after dark.

Shaded by coco palms and bordered by lush tropical

plants. Lanikūhonua is, by day, a cultural center where Hawaiian language and crafts are taught along with ancient *kahiko* hula. Lanikūhonua is one of the few places in the state with an ancient-style *pā hula*, a grassy earth platform for dancing. There are *heiau* and other stone platforms.

Once the weekend retreat for Alice Kamokila Campbell, heir to the Campbell estate, the Lanikūhonua Cultural Institute was established after her death to promote the Hawaiian way. The institute apparently has done an excellent job.

Although I have never personally experienced anything out of the ordinary after dark at Lanikūhonua, I am told the place is haunted by wandering spirits who cause great mischief but no harm. You should go and see for yourself.

Moana Hotel Room 120

On February 28, 1905, Jane Stanford, the millionairess widow of Stanford University founder Sen. Leland Stanford, toured Oʻahu, ate a picnic lunch in a grove of trees over the Pali, paid her respects to Hawaiʻi's deceased kings and queens at the Royal Mausoleum, and then returned to the Moana Hotel, where she had a bowl of soup for dinner, took a beach walk and went to bed at 8:30 P.M.

About 10 P.M., Mrs. Stanford was found, holding her stomach, leaning against her bedroom door, crying out: "Bertha! Mae!" she said. "I am so sick!" Dr. J. H. Humphris, the hotel's resident physician, arrived to find the woman suffering convulsions.

"Doctor, I think I am poisoned!" she said. "Oh God, forgive me my sins! This is a horrible death to die!"

She died at 11:40 P.M. in her room. Her death was

attributed to strychnine poisoning. Stanford University officials, however, claimed she died of heart failure. To this day, mystery surrounds the death of Mrs. Stanford, another of Hawai'i's unsolved mysteries.

You can book Jane Stanford's room at the Moana Hotel and spend the night, but bring your own soup.

MAUI

Ke'anae Peninsula

On the winding road to Hāna the old Hawaiian village of Ke'anae stands out in the Pacific like a place time forgot. Here, on an old lava flow graced by an 1860 stone church and swaying palms, is one of the last coastal enclaves of Native Hawaiians. It's a very spiritual place. A few Hawaiians still grow taro in patches and pound it into poi, the staple of the old diet. Some still pluck *'opihi* (shellfish) from tidepools along the jagged coast and cast throw nets at schools of fish. The remnants of a lost culture. I always feel haunted here by what might have been.

Pu'u Kukui

I am standing near the 5,871-foot summit of Pu'u Kukui ("hill of enlightenment") in the West Maui Mountains, which early Hawaiians believed to be the junction between heaven and earth.

It is easy to see why: up here the peaks are often wreathed in clouds and pierced by gold rays of the sun. 'Iao Valley and Haleakalā are awesome, but Pu'u Kukui is heavenly.

You can visit this 10-million-year-old cloud forest now by helicopter (thanks to the nonprofit Kapalua Nature Society) if you are one of twelve lucky people to win a ticket. Long *kapu* to all but scientists, the forest is one of the last native forests in Hawai'i, and it is biologically rich with flora and fauna.

A narrow boardwalk edges through the 8,661-acre upland bog, which is a wonderland of spiky silverswords and unassuming sedges, rare daisies, wild orchids, and giant *hāpu'u* ferns. Bright red dragonflies flit above true blue Lake Violet. Thick shawls of moss drape dwarf *'ōhi'a* trees.

I never spotted the three native birds—the *'i'iwi*, *'apapane*, and *'amakihi*—that live here, but watched miniature Hawaiian land snails, each a different stripe and color, slide up and down leggy stalks of the rare *Brighamia insignia*, an Alice in Wonderland plant that looks like a cabbage on a baseball bat.

And there at heaven's gate I did see the seldom-seen Gloria Mantis plant, commonly called "the glory of the mountain." It resembles an artichoke crossed with a gladiolus and grows like a beanstalk eight feet tall.

Kahakuloa Valley

All valleys in Hawai'i are spooky, especially after dark. Hālawa Valley on Moloka'i is haunted by a *mo'o* lizard. Nenewe, the Shark Man, lives in a pool in Waipi'o Valley on the Big Island of Hawai'i. Even fairly civilized Mānoa Valley in Honolulu is haunted. Just ask any University of Hawai'i student who lives in the dorms.

When you want to really experience chicken skin, you must go to Maui's Kahakuloa Valley on the raw northwestern shore, where the pavement runs out and the road narrows to one lane.

Deep in Kahakuloa Valley you can walk in the footsteps of night marchers, visit the mysterious C-shaped structures, hear Oliver Dukelow tell the old "talk stories" handed down through the generations.

Lindbergh's Grave

Charles A. Lindbergh, the first aviator to fly solo across the Atlantic, lies buried in a grave he designed in the churchyard of century-old Palapala Ho'omau Congregational Church in Kīpahulu, Maui.

The grave, built according to Lindbergh's sketches, is eight feet square, twelve feet deep, with walls of lava rock. A large piece of granite is covered with loose, smooth, round *'ili'ili* (small stones), in the Hawaiian tradition.

Lindbergh was buried in a casket made of eucalyptus and lined with a Hudson's Bay blanket that he had been given by his mother; a cushion from his plane, the *Spirit of St. Louis*, to be placed under his body; and a Hawaiian tapa cloth covering for his body. He was buried barefoot in khaki clothes. His grave is inscribed, "Charles Lindbergh Died Maui 1974," with Verse 9 of Psalm 139:

"If I take the wings of the morning and dwell in the uttermost part of the sea . . . "

Hundreds of curious visit Lindbergh's grave each year. Some bring him hibiscus and plumeria blossoms, others take *'ilil'ili* from his grave as token souvenirs.

Wailua River State Park

Ancients called the Wailua River "Wailua Nui a Hōano," the river of the great sacred spirit. Seven sacred temples once stood along the twenty-mile river fed by 5,148-foot Mt. Wai'ale'ale, the wettest spot on earth—it gets forty feet of rain a year and is the source of Kaua'i's waterfalls, rivers, and great green look.

If you go up Hawai'i's only navigable river by boat, or drive The King's Highway, which goes inland along the river, you will enter this sacred, historical place believed founded by Puna, a Tahitian priest who arrived in one of the first migrations, declared Kaua'i his kingdom, and put everything in sight under a *kapu*.

Here in this royal settlement are remains of the seven temples, including a sacrificial *heiau*, a place of refuge and a planetarium, the royal birthing stones, and a stone bell to announce a royal birth.

Go up Wailua River by kayak or boat, or drive The King's Highway, which goes inland along the river, to enter this sacred, historical place.

Mt. Wai'ale'ale

There's something otherworldly about Wai'ale'ale, the 5,148-foot peak on the island of Kaua'i. Ancient Hawaiians built a *heiau* on Wai'ale'ale, which means "rippling or overflowing water," and no doubt prayed to stop the rain.

Wai'ale'ale is, after all, the wettest place on earth.

A collapsed caldera, this multipronged cloud-catcher sends world record torrents down Kaua'i's seven rivers to keep the Garden Island green. Up there, it rains daily, year 'round. Since 1910, the U.S. Geologic Survey has measured the rainfall. Records show it rains 435 inches (37 feet) a year. One year it rained 950 inches, or almost 80 feet.

I go as often as I can on a bumpy helicopter ride to see the earth's wettest spot, not always with great success. Once, all I saw was the inside of a storm cloud. On another rare sunny day, the waterfalls showed as bone-dry grooves. But one rainy day, the clouds parted only for a moment to reveal in brilliant sunshine the full spectacle of Wai'ale'ale's raw nature—countless icy blue waterfalls lacing the spiky green velvet cathedral-like peaks of the rust red volcano. It was like gazing upon a lost kingdom in the sky.

MOLOKA'I

Pu'u Ka'ana (see page 84)

LĀNA'I

Luahiwa Petroglyphs

I sat in full sun, all alone on the steep hillside overlooking the broad caldera known as Pālāwai Basin, studying petroglyphs one afternoon on Lāna'i. That's the best time of day to see the stone age art, because the sun lights up the indented stick figures.

It's an amazing cast of characters unlike any on Lāna'i or any other island for that matter. The first time I visited Luahiwa Petroglyphs it was raining so hard I couldn't even see the twenty boulders bearing stone-age artwork. So I returned the following year on a hot August day. I climbed up the hillside through the bone-dry brush and, a little out of breath, sat down amid the petroglyph boulders. Maybe it was the heat, or my imagination, but the pictures came alive and seemed to move as if in an early cartoon.

I saw a canoe sail cruise across the face of a gigantic red boulder, saw a curly-tailed dog bark at a centipede, and a horseman with a hat riding a thin horse while two V-chested men walked down a trail. I even saw two turtles inch across the rock. Or thought I did. That's when I felt an icy shiver in the hot afternoon and decided to go. I also thought it better then not to tell anybody about what I'd seen. Back at the Lodge, when the young Hawaiian woman who serves as concierge asked about my visit with the petroglyphs, I smiled and said they were wonderful and that she should go see them someday. She winced and shivered and said, "Too spooky, yeah?"

BIG ISLAND

The King's Trail (see page 109)

Captain Cook's Monument, Kealakekua Bay

In 1861 King Kamehameha IV said his kingdom possessed only two things worth visiting—Kīlauea volcano and the spot on Kealakekua Bay where Capt. James Cook met his death in 1779.

Nearly two million people visit the volcano each year, while few pay their respects to Captain Cook, who was killed on February 14, 1779, the day of "the fatal catastrophe," as British historians say. The murder site remained "haunted" for nearly forty years; no European captains dared sail to Hawai'i.

A stark white concrete obelisk stands onshore in memory of the man who charted the Pacific on three voyages between 1768 and 1778. A bronze plaque at the base of the monument reads:

"In memory of the great circumnavigator, Capt. James Cook, RN, who discovered these islands on the 18th day of January AD 1778 and fell near this spot on the 14th day of February AD 1779."

The death site was deeded to England for $1 by a Hawaiian princess in 1877, "to keep and maintain . . . a monument in memory of Captain Cook." British sailors come ashore once a year to whitewash the obelisk.

I always get a little chicken skin here when I imagine the blue, blue water running deep and red with blood on one of those perfect days in paradise.

David Douglas Memorial

Near the 7,000-foot elevation of Mauna Kea on the Big Island of Hawai'i stands an incongruous ring of Douglas fir trees around an eight-foot pyramid of stones with a brass plate that reads:

KALUAKAUKA
In Memory of
Dr. David Douglas
Killed Near This Spot
In A Wild Bullock Pit
July 12, 1834 A.D.

A botanical collector for England's Royal Horticultural Society, and namesake of the Douglas fir, he met his demise on his way to Hilo with a satchel of cash under mysterious circumstances. His body was found in a lava pit used to trap wild bulls. He was 35.

Douglas was last seen by a wrangler named Edward Gurney, an ex-convict from England. He said he found Douglas in the pit with a bull, which he slew. The money never was found, and Douglas's head bore suspicious wounds. Foul play was suspected. Gurney quit Hawai'i for California's gold rush, never to be heard from again.

Fellow botanists planted Douglas firs and erected the monument to Douglas in Hakalau Wilderness Preserve. His tombstone reposes in Kawaiaha'o Church's vestibule. His death remains unsolved.

Kazumura Cave

Hawai'i's biggest known cave, the Kazumura Cave is 29.32 miles long with 50-foot-high chambers, shark-tooth stalactites, and crawl passages so small only one person can squeeze through at a time.

If you're afraid of the dark, or small spaces, don't go here. Extremes of claustrophobia and agoraphobia can be experienced fifty feet under the earth's surface in this the biggest lava tube cavern ever found in the islands.

The spooky cave, fully explored and measured only in 1993 by spelunkers Kevin and Carleen Allred of Alaska, has an ecosystem all its own; it is home to a small white leaf hopper with a waxy convex white tail that thrives on the long, wispy roots of 'ōhi'a trees. No ali'i bones, feathered capes, fishhooks, or canoe relics were found, however.

The subterranean passage, which could be Hawai'i's answer to Carlsbad Caverns, is all under private land and requires special permission to enter. At your own risk.